Hold me

A GREENGROVE NOVEL

Produced by Softwood Books, Suffolk, UK

Printed and bound in Great Britain by TJ Books Limited, Padstow, Cornwall

Text © Helen Kelly

First Edition

ISBN: 978-1-7396074-6-3

www.softwoodbooks.com

Dedication

I have a passion for writing about strong women, and sadly, our family had to bid farewell to three remarkable women in 2023. As a result, this book is dedicated to them.

Acknowledgement

I would like to thank my friends and family for all the help and support you have given me while I have continued on my author's journey. This year has been very difficult, but together we have got through it.

Prologue

Dawn

It was hard to work out how these symptoms had started. It was like a really bad flu that never went away. I will never forget the conversation I had with my twin sister Debbie nine months ago when she finally sat me down and told me a few home truths.

I had a really bad week. The pain was awful, and I was taking over the counter tablets to the maximum, but they just weren't doing anything. All they seemed to do was make me tired, but that didn't stop the pain. Opening my front door with her key, Debbie shouted, "Where are you? I have brought dinner. There is something I need to talk to you about."

"Just coming." Walking slowly from the bedroom where I had been lying down, I went to the living room, where my sister was just putting up some place mats on the coffee table in front of the sofa for what turned out to be our shared Chinese dinner. Luckily, she hadn't bought a lot, because I wasn't hungry. I tried to smile at her, although even that seemed to take too much energy.

"I bought a few of your favourites. I thought we would have them and then talk, if that's okay."

"Of course. It's nothing serious, is it? You are okay, aren't you?"

"There's nothing to worry about. I just want to put an idea to you"

"Oh, that's good."

While we ate our dinner we talked about her upcoming shifts at the hospital and my work as an assistant project manager. I had just heard that they had confirmed that they wanted everyone to continue working from home unless there were special meetings and specific projects that required us to meet on-site. It was something I had been hoping for, because I was worried about how I was going to manage going to the office every day at the moment. Dinner was finished, and Debbie cleared up and made us both a drink before sitting down on the sofa next to me. Reaching for my hand, she said, "I don't want you to be upset with me because I have been worried about you. I know you haven't been yourself, and my twinny sense is going mad. That tingle I get in my shoulder blade that tells me there is something wrong is going off all the time, so I have started writing a diary."

"I have tried not to worry you."

"I know, but I think the time has come for you to go to see Doctor Davies. This has been going on for too long, and you're not getting any better. In fact, I don't think you even realise it, but I think you are getting worse."

"I know I am getting weaker, and knackered even though I haven't done anything special."

"That's what I thought."

"Okay, I will make an appointment with Dr Davies tomorrow. Do you want to share what you have noticed?"

We went through Debbie's diary, and although some of it made both of us cry, as it pointed out the realistic situation of my life and things I had been ignoring or had decided were nothing, I knew she was right. So the next day I made an appointment to see the doctor.

I managed to get an appointment a week later. I told the receptionist it wasn't urgent. Debbie wasn't happy about that, because her view was that it was urgent, as it had been going on for too long, whereas my view was that it wasn't urgent for the same reason.

I drove to my appointment. Even though the surgery was only a five minute walk from my house, there was no way I could have walked. The waiting room was only small, because the doctor's surgery was actually a converted cottage. The doctor's waiting room was the front room, with his consulting room in the dining room and the reception room in the hall. There were some other consulting rooms, and the garage had been converted into one of the nurses' rooms. The others were upstairs. Most of the villagers had been coming there since they'd been born. Well, at least those my age. No sooner had I sat down than Dr Davies called me in. Dr Davies was the only Doctor I remembered. He always walked into the waiting room smiling at everyone who was there to see him. Although he had shrunk a bit through old age like everyone does, he still reminded me of a cuddly grandad; someone who you would trust to keep you and your secrets safe.

Walking into his consulting room, I sat down, and we smiled at him.

"Hello, Dawn. What can I do for you?"

"I am sorry to bother you, but Debbie was insistent that I came to see you. About a month ago I think I started getting what I can only describe as flu-like symptoms, but they haven't really gone away."

"I am glad you have come to see me. So, let's go through a few of the normal tests—blood pressure, temperature, oxygen levels, and such—while you tell me some of your symptoms."

"Okay. I have aching joints and tiredness. My body feels heavy. I am uncoordinated. I forget things. I have sensitivity to things that shouldn't be painful. Sometimes, if someone just passes too close by and nudges me, it feels as if they had slapped me. I can't sleep, despite being tired. Nothing really makes sense."

Whilst I was explaining what had been happening to me Dr Davies did his checks.

"Everything is normal. I want you to have some blood tests. I take it you have tried over-the-counter painkillers and they didn't work?"

"Yes, I did, and no, they didn't touch the pain at all."

"Right. There are a few options we can try. Unfortunately, it will be trial and error until we can get to the root of the problem, but at least you have been to see me now."

"Alright."

"Here's a prescription for some painkillers. Try these for a month. Here is your blood test appointment. Someone will phone you with the results a week after the test, and I want you to make an appointment for a month after starting these tablets. Is that alright?"

"Yes, thank you."

"If there are any problems, I want you to come back and see me sooner."

"I will, I promise. Thank you."

Since that first appointment all those months ago, things never improved; in fact, they just got worse. I had to explain to Dr Davies on one of my many consultations that:

"The pain comes out of nowhere. It started simply with tingling in my hands, then, as time went on, it developed into all-over body pain, which started with just a dull ache like I explained to you the first time I came to see you and has developed into a searing pain. No two days are the same. I have tried to keep a diary, but honestly, it began to look like a work of fiction. I am starting to feel depressed over what I can and can't do. I hardly leave the house now. Debbie takes me shopping on a Saturday when she's not working, but sometimes even that is a struggle."

"I know this is hard, Dawn, and every test we try is coming back negative, but we are trying to find an answer. I do believe that there is something wrong with you, we just need to find out what, and I am sorry it is taking so long. I want to book you in for an MRI at the hospital. It has been a while since your bloods have been taken. I want to see if your inflammation markers have changed, so we can repeat those as well. What about those pain killers? Were they any better?"

"No, just the same, only this time instead of making me spaced out they affected my stomach, so like last time, I stopped them straight away."

"Good, so the plan is going to be that you will hear from the hospital with an MRI date. Go and have your blood tests and I will prescribe you another painkiller. These ones shouldn't affect your stomach, but don't try them for another two weeks. That should give the others time to leave your system. Are you alright with that?"

"Yes, thank you."

Two Months Later

Today's appointment at the doctors was at 2.30, and my twin sister, Debbie, said she would come with me. I think she was almost more worried than I was, as today we would be getting the results from the MRI.

I'd spent most of the day working from home. I was just saving my work when I heard Debbie let herself in. We both had keys to each other's houses, but Debbie had started using hers every time she came to mine to save me from getting up. It was especially handy when I was engrossed in work. Once, before she'd started using her key on a regular basis and only had it for emergencies, she'd knocked on the door while I was in a online meeting. I had ignored it, thinking it wasn't important, then when I'd come off the meeting I forgot to check and didn't realise she had still been there. The thing had been, she had locked herself out of her house without her phone or keys or purse. Because she couldn't get an answer, she had decided to be resourceful and gone to the pub. Instead of getting our friend James, who owns the pub, to lend her his phone, she had persuaded him to start a tab and had been considerate enough to let me finish work before she'd asked him to phone me to come and get her. That had been nearly two years ago, and she still hadn't paid me back for the bar bill.

"Don't worry, it's only me," I heard her shout, as she so often did.

"I'll be right there. I'm just finishing work."

"No problem."

The moment I got downstairs, she said, "I know you're going to complain, but I thought we would walk to the surgery. If we take the shortcut, it should only take five minutes."

"I'm not sure, I'm a bit tired already. I'll be wiped out, and then I have to walk back."

"I think that it's a good thing, you going to the doctor exhausted. It will help him see what we are talking about, and if you can't walk back, I promise to come back for the car while you wait at the surgery."

I sighed. "All right. I'll give it a go."

"I don't want you to walk if you think it will be too much for you, if you don't try, you'll be disappointed in yourself. I am your twin, after all. I know you quite well."

I groaned. It was always annoying when she was right.

Using my walking stick, and with the help of Dawn, we got to the surgery in time for my appointment. I was relieved when we got there. Gasping for breath, my chest heaving, my muscles aching, my body shaking, I practically creaked as I sat down in the waiting room. Debbie helped me get up off the chair and walk into his room. Each time I was in his room I could not help but be hit by the fact that, like him his room, hadn't changed much over time. It still had the old wooden desk I remembered playing under when my mum used to bring us when we were children, and a picture of his now-grown-up children, which had changed over time, remained in the same frame he'd put them in when his firstborn had arrived.

"Take a seat, ladies."

Debbie helped me sit down before she took her own seat.

Dr Davies turned to me. "Dawn, is it okay to discuss everything in front of Debbie?"

"Yes, that's fine."

"Good. Now, your blood tests have all come back with normal levels. As you know, the X-rays and MRI tests all came back clear, so they haven't shown up any reason for your symptoms."

"I'm not imagining the pain and fatigue. All we did to get here was a little walk through the cut and I'm breathless, washed out, and my body is painful, and that is just the tip of the iceberg. This is not normal for someone my age."

"I agree with you, Dawn. I know it's not in your imagination. I think you have a condition called fibromyalgia. I will, however, need to request a rheumatologist's report just to make sure that they agree with me."

I didn't know what to say. At last, I might have had a reason for why I was feeling this way.

"What is fibromyalgia?" Debbie asked.

"Fibromyalgia is a long-term pain condition that has various symptoms other than pain, most of which Dawn has been suffering. For example, increased sensitivity, muscle stiffness, difficulty with sleep, brain fog, headaches, irritable bowel, frustration, low moods. These symptoms are changeable and can get suddenly worse. They call it a flare-up. Unfortunately, it's a long-term condition. I have printed off a leaflet which explains the condition. There are also a few websites which can help. Fibromyalgia Action UK and Versus Arthritis are good places to look. I also want you to know that you can always come to me or anyone at the surgery if you have any questions."

"Thank you. So, what happens now? If it is fibromyalgia, can it be cured?" Debbie always knew the right thing to ask.

"I will send the referral to the hospital. Hopefully, there won't be too long to wait before you see the rheumatologist. Unfortunately, there is no cure for fibromyalgia; it's just a case of managing it. There are some things we can do to make the symptoms better, most of which we have already tried for you, but they didn't seem to work with your symptoms. If the consultant agrees that it is fibromyalgia, then we can refer you to a specialist clinic that will be able to help further. I don't know how long the wait will be before you hear from the hospital, but until then, the only thing we can do is try to find some painkillers that help. With that in mind, how have you been getting on with the tablets I gave you last time? Do they help?"

"They do a little bit, but they make me feel lightheaded, which means I'm frightened to drive anywhere, and work is becoming a challenge."

"That's not good. I think it might be worthwhile for you to come off those tablets, but we will need to wean you off them over the next month, so we will need to wait for a month before we can see if there is anything else you can take. Until then, just take paracetamol as and when you need it. I know that's not much help, but I think it's best if you stop the most recent set of pain meds, especially if the side effects affect your normal day-to-day activities. I also want you to come back in another month to see me, but if you need me before that, you know where I am."

"Okay, thank you." With that, we left his office.

Shoulders slumped and head hung low, I traipsed back to the waiting room.

"Are you okay?" Debbie asked.

I sighed. "Well, I'd hoped that there might be a name for what I had. At least it means I'm not going mad, but ... there's no cure, is there?

Debbie frowned. "It's just a case of managing it, I think."

I sank down onto a waiting room chair, staring at the white wall before me.

"You sit here. I'm going to get the car and will come and pick you up ... because you look done in," Debbie said.

"Thank you. I don't know what I would do without you."

"That's because I'm the best twin sister a person could ask for. I won't be long."

She was right. She was the best sister a person could ever have. When we got back to my house, she followed me in and made us both a cup of tea.

"How do you feel?"

"I don't know, sis." I rubbed my eyes and looked at the steaming mug before me on the kitchen table. "I'm relieved that I didn't make up the pain, but … I'm worried about the future and what all this will mean. How can I have a husband and family … like this? I mean, who would want me when I can't even walk five minutes to the doctor's?"

"It's not the end of your life. Some things will change, yes, but other people will have found a way around it. I know it's easier for me to look at the positives, but … let's look on the internet. There might be more advice."

"Okay."

And that was what we did, long into the evening at my office desk, only stopping to order a takeaway and eat. There was quite a lot of information online, with some positive stories, and negative, but with all the research we had done, what I did realised was that it affected people differently and no two people had the same experiences. I supposed that was why it was difficult to diagnose and treat.

"Look here." Debbie read a passage out loud, peering at

the computer screen from over my shoulder. "As soon as the diagnosis is confirmed, help can be given for physiotherapy and plans can be developed to help you manage the condition. That's positive!"

I really wanted to believe her, that it would be that easy.

It took six months before I had my next hospital appointment, and it was only a telephone appointment. After asking me some questions, the consultant said that they agreed with Dr Davies's diagnosis of fibromyalgia. Soon after, I was referred to the fibromyalgia clinic, who offered various services, including a physiotherapist, who helped by giving me some exercises that I could do to try and keep my body healthy, and a therapist who helped me come to terms with my condition and how I felt about what was a new stage in my life.

I had been offered a choice of face-to-face or video therapy appointments. I chose video ones, because I had decided to give up driving as I was finding it difficult concentrating on the road and was normally exhausted by the time I got anywhere after driving and was in the process of selling my car.

My first appointment was good, although I was nervous, as I didn't know what to expect. Even though we were only going to be meeting through a computer screen, it took me a while to put in the right password to access the desktop on my laptop because my hands were shaking so much. I had to keep trying to slow my breathing down, as I was worried I was going to have a panic attack, and I could feel all the muscles in my neck tense up. Having negotiated the virtual waiting room, I was in the middle of holding my breath when I was 'let in', so the first view she had of me was when I rushed a breath out and choked. Once I'd recovered, we introduced ourselves, and the therapist asked me to explain what having Fibromyalgia meant to me.

"To be honest, it's difficult to explain. I am relieved that I finally have a diagnosis and that there is something wrong with me, but on the other side, I feel like a failure, because there is so much now that I can't do that I used to be able to do."

"This is a common feeling for someone who has just been diagnosed, and unfortunately, because it's a lifelong condition that relies on management rather than cure, there are times when these feelings of failure will be strong, especially when you are having a flare, so it is important to listen to your body and talk to your friends and family."

"I don't like relying on my sister too much. She has her own life; she doesn't want to be stuck looking after me all the time. I don't want to hold her back because I can't do something that she wants to do."

"This is where communication is important. I bet she won't feel the way you think she does. If you thought she was going through the things that you are going through, would you feel that you were stuck with her and she was holding you back?"

"No."

"Well then, why would you think that she would think that about you?"

"That's true, she is forever telling me I am not a failure and that I need to stop apologising. Obviously, I needed to hear it from someone else before I could look at it from a different side."

I had ten appointments in total with the therapist. She helped me to realise that having fibromyalgia was going to be a rollercoaster, with no two days the same, but that I had to listen to my body and accept, no matter how hard it was, that I couldn't overdo things. It also taught me systems that would help me overcome and manage the dark feelings that would appear, especially during a flare-up. At those moments, I needed to ask for help—especially from those who were willing to help—and to not be too hard on myself.

Chapter 1

One year later

Dawn

"Knock knock!" I heard Debbie call out as she walked into the spare room which I had converted into my office.

"Hi. I didn't expect to see you today. What's up?"

"I thought I would bring you some dinner. You sounded exhausted when I spoke to you this morning. What are you doing still working?"

"I was really tired this morning, so I started at lunchtime when I had recovered a bit." That cost me one spoon. "Luckily, today's work didn't require too much concentration. I appreciate you bringing me dinner. Are you staying for some?"

"Yeah, if that's okay." Another spoon gone. "Also, I wanted to talk to you about something."

"Okay, let me just finish off here. I'll be another ten minutes or so, is that okay?" How many spoons did I have left for the day?

"Of course, I'll go put dinner in the oven to warm. Don't rush."

Since going to the fibromyalgia clinic, I had learnt to measure my life in spoons. The theory: someone with a chronic illness starts each day with a certain number of spoons and each thing they do uses up a spoon, so it is quite easy to run out of spoons.

It took me a little bit longer than I had thought to finish off, and by the time I went into the kitchen, Debbie had put my washing on, folded up the linen from the tumble dryer, and set the table. I sat down while Debbie got a lasagne out of the oven and put it on the mat in the middle of the table. She had also brought a salad and some garlic bread.

"Help yourself," she said with a smile.

"Thanks. I'll eat as much as I can," I replied. "Last week was … difficult."

"Yes, the work conference. How did it go?"

"I was fine, it was fine … but I'm paying for it now." Fatigue, pain … all the symptoms I had grown used to.

"You shouldn't push yourself to hard. I'm here to help you whenever."

"I know. And I appreciate you doing all of this …" I waved my hand around the room, "…but you know you don't have to. I will get around to it when I can."

"I know I don't, but it gave me something to do, and you know me, I'm the weird one who enjoys folding up clothes. You are the normal one, putting it off until you simply can't anymore."

I laughed at the twinkle in her eye. She felt wanted, and I felt looked after. It worked well enough.

We ate our lasagne, talking about the conference I had been to and its aftereffects on my health. Talking to people I hadn't met before, or even those I hadn't seen for a while, staying in a hotel where the conferences were taking place, had meant that people always wanted to talk about work matters, even during dinner, so there hadn't really been any time to turn my brain off. It wasn't just mentally exhausting, physically too.

When our plates were clear, Debbie put the leftovers in the fridge and, together, we put the dishwasher on before going into the living room.

"I'm worried about you, Dawn. You work from home as much as you can, and other than when I take you shopping, you don't leave the house."

"I am okay, honestly. I went to the gala evening at the community centre the other month."

"That was over a year ago, and before you got your diagnosis." Debbie gave me a stern look.

"I didn't think it was that long ago."

"It was, and even then, you hardly spoke to anyone."

"I wasn't well that night, if you remember. It was right at the beginning of my condition, and I was in so much pain I could hardly stand. And I did talk to those on our table."

"I bet you don't even remember who they were."

"Well, no. Who were they?"

"We were sitting at the table that you had managed to fill with your work colleagues. You had convinced your boss that it would be a good idea to support the village, where a large percentage of his clients come from."

"I don't remember that at all."

"I know. Look, I know how hard it is for you to go out, and you are getting better at managing things, but I think it would do you some good to get out more and be amongst people who know you and knew you before your illness. Please."

"Well, we can go to the pub if you want or, for our birthday, we could see if we could get a table at the Fish by the River."

"That's a good idea, but that's not what I was thinking about."

"Oh, so what do you mean?"

"You know Jane restarted the choir … I thought you could go to that?"

"Are you kidding me? How am I going to manage being in a choir? People don't realise how much energy that would entail. I wouldn't be able to stand up and sing."

"Calm down. I have spoken to Jane about your condition, and she said that she would love you to be in the choir, sitting or standing. The next rehearsal is on Thursday evening. She'll help wherever she can so that you're comfortable."

"I can't believe this. You spoke to Jane without my permission. I don't want everyone to know my business." I looked away from her, my chest tightening. "I need you to leave. I'm too tired to deal with this at the moment."

I couldn't look her in the eye. How could she force me into something like that? Of all people, I thought she understood.

"And there's that stubborn look again." She shook her head. "I want you to remember that I am not the enemy here. I love you, and I am trying to do what I can to help you get back to having a social life and to be the Dawn you used to be. You need to control this condition. Don't let it control you. I'll phone you later."

When the front door closed behind her, my heart lurched. I fought back tears as I used up my last energy spoon of the day and put everything away in the kitchen. I was so tired after that, I just decided to go to bed.

But I couldn't sleep. Not from the usual pain; my conversation with Debbie just wouldn't leave my mind. I knew deep down that she was right, but the thought of facing other people and pretending to be strong … I didn't want to face their pity when they saw me struggling to stand. What would they think? Would people think I was making it up? No one could see the pain. I'd got odd looks before when going the supermarket and parking in Blue Badge parking spaces. Someone had once confronted me, saying "You can't park there. That is for disabled people." I'd cried for hours. It just didn't look like there was anything wrong with me.

Debbie rang that night as I was tossing and turning, and I had a quick brief talk with her, but I was still cross.

The next morning, I was sitting at my desk, working on inputting data into spreadsheets. My phone rang whilst I was finishing off the column I was on.

"Hi Dawn, it's Jane."

"Hello."

"I wondered if it would be possible to pop around and see you tonight for a chat?"

I sighed to myself. "Yes, of course."

"That's great. What time would be best for you?"

"If you come around any time after five, I will have finished work."

The rest of the day passed by quickly. I had heard from Debbie via text, but I knew I wouldn't see her that night because she was working on the children's ward. My musings during the night meant that I was no longer angry with her and I could understand what she'd meant, especially when I thought about how long it had been since I had been out socially. So, maybe she had had a point, and if I had been in the same position as her, I would have said the same, though I may have been even more stubborn.

Jane sent me a text to let me know she was on her way round just after five, and it only took ten minutes for her to get to my house.

There was a knock on the door and, as expected, Jane was on the other side. Smiling at me, she hugged me and told me I was looking well.

"Thank you. Please come in."

As I'd had a bit more energy, I had done a few jobs in the house before she'd arrived, so the living room was nice and tidy.

"Would you like a drink?"

"Just a glass of tap water would be wonderful, thank you."

"Of course."

As soon as I sat down with our drinks, Jane said, "Dawn, I have known you a long time. We are friends who came through all the problems with Sarah together. I am sorry I didn't realise that you were having health problems."

"I wish I had known about the problems you were having with Peter. I would have helped you in any way I could."

"We are a right pair! We're often too busy trying to survive with everything that is being thrown at us."

"How is that wonderful fiancé of yours, David?"

"He's perfect, only don't tell him that!" she laughed. "You are coming to the wedding, aren't you?"

"I'm looking forward to it." Though I really don't know how I'll manage.

"I can't believe that it's only a month away. The time has gone so fast. Anyway, I think you can guess why I wanted to come round and see you."

"You have spoken to Debbie."

"She's worried about you, and, honestly, if I hadn't been so caught up with my problems, I would be worried about you too. In the interest of honesty, I want you to know I spoke to Debbie this morning before I rang you, and I know that you had words last night."

"Well … I've had a chance to calm down and think … and I know she's right, however annoying that is. I do need to get out of the house more and meet people."

"That's what I needed to hear. I didn't want to get my stern teacher voice out. I had put it away for the day when I finished work. But I want to know what I can do to help you enjoy yourself. I did some research on fibromyalgia, so I know the mechanics of what it is, but nowhere could I find where it says what I can do to help you. So tell me, please."

"I appreciate you trying to help, but until I come along and see how it affects me, I won't know really what will help. Does that make sense?"

"Yes, it does. From what I had read, you need things like regular breaks and not too much stress."

"I can't believe you went to all the trouble to research this!"

"Of course I did! That's what friends are for!"

"Thank you."

"No thanks required, but I did have an idea. Why don't you come along on Thursday night and see what you think about singing? You could sing one or two songs, but you don't need to sing them all. There are a few people in the choir that don't sing all the songs because they just don't like the song. If you don't think you can manage the singing, you can just come down and help me manage it. Trust me, the adults are worse than the kids when it comes to organisation." They both chuckled.

"That sounds great. As long as you're sure I won't be in your way. I'm still a little bit nervous about being out and about, but Debbie said she would bring me … though, as you well know, you don't want her singing."

"Oh, help." Jane gave me a look of embarrassment. "I remember when she decided she wanted to audition for the part of Sandy in the school's production of Grease because she wanted to kiss the boy who played Danny. I don't think Mr Spencer's hearing was ever the same again after that."

"Everyone else got off mildly. Some of us had to share a room with her at home, and she practised whenever she could, but even she admitted she couldn't sing. But she was willing to do anything to get that kiss. After her audition, the boy, whose name I can't remember, didn't speak to her ever again. But in her own Debbie way, she's made a joke of it, and whenever someone annoys her she'll ask them if they want her to sing them a song."

"I remember her doing that in school! And the way people went pale and ran away. It was like her superpower."

The memories we shared lightened up the atmosphere in the room, and by the time Jane left, my mood had lifted. It was like no time had passed at all. I promised her that I would come to the choir practice on Thursday and that if I needed anything, I would let her know.

I also sent Debbie a text.

"I am sorry I overreacted yesterday. Jane has just left, and we have sorted some things out so that I can go on Thursday without any problems."

As soon as she had read the text, she rang me.

"You're forgiven," she told me.

"Thank you. I told Jane I would come on Thursday. Is it still okay for you to take me? Otherwise she said she would pick me up."

"Nope, I am taking you. I know it's only two days away, but I don't want you to change your mind."

"Okay, thank you. What plans do you have tomorrow?"

"Not a lot after work. I need to pop to the shops, so if you want anything, let me know. Other than that, nothing."

"I don't think I need anything. I have leftovers for tonight and some salad for tomorrow."

"Good. I hope you rest tomorrow evening so that you aren't too tired for Thursday."

"I'm not going to do much tomorrow. As you said, I need to conserve my energy." Time to store up my spoons.

"Okay, well if you can think of anything you need, just send me a text. I need to go. I've just finished my break and I need to let you go so you can get your dinner then go to bed. Love you and see you Thursday."

"Love you too, sis."

Connor

The pub was so busy, James and I could hardly hear each other speak.

"I just need to –" James stood up from our table.

"No, James! It's your night off!" I pushed him back into his seat. "Your staff are fine. They don't need your help tonight."

"Fine. Fine."

"How are the wedding plans coming along?" I asked with a grin, fully expecting his predictable response.

"Oh, not you as well! I just wanted one night away from frilly gowns and table décor," James groaned. "It's all Lacy and Jane seem to talk about nowadays."

Like many people in Greengrove, I had known James all my life. We'd been best friends since school. He was now married to the love of his life, Lacy, and his cousin Jane was getting married to his friend David in just over a month. I had met him once or twice. A decent man. Completely in love with Jane. He'd moved to the village a few years ago, but he fit in so well, you wouldn't know he hadn't grown up here like the rest of us.

James had already bought two rounds, which was unusual, so he obviously wanted something. I was going to see how long I could plead ignorance to his plan and see how many drinks I could get out of him. It was unusual for him to voluntarily put his hand in his pocket. However, curiosity got the better of me, so when he passed me my third drink, I asked him.

"I give up. What do you want? What causes a man to buy three drinks in a pub when normally he moans about buying one?"

"Who said I want anything?"

"Come off it, James! I have known you all my life. I know when you want me to do something for you that you don't think I will like."

"Damn, I never could fool you."

"No, you couldn't. So spit it out before I ask for a double whiskey for the next round instead of this pint of bitter."

"Fine. So … do you remember in school when you used to be in the choir?"

"No."

"You must do?"

"I mean, no, I am not doing it."

"I haven't even asked yet."

"You don't need to. You want me to put my name down for choir in the community centre."

"Okay, well, maybe. I was more obvious than I wanted to be."

"You were?"

"Okay, well, the problem is that Jane is stressed at the moment with the wedding planning, work at the school, and the choir. Mum is worried about her, and I know David is trying to help her as well, but I made the stupid mistake of asking her if I could help in any way, and she said it would be a good help if I could persuade you to be in the choir. So I said without thinking, of course, no problem, to which Jane kept saying thank you as if I had just made her a millionaire. That's why I am here—well, that and of course your wonderful company … and to get away from the endless talk about weddings."

"Flattering. Why does she want me in the choir?"

"She is short of men. I offered, but she said I don't have the skills required. I think that's code for 'You haven't got a great singing voice'."

"Well, to be honest, you haven't."

"Unlike you, which is why Jane needs you."

"Look, I like Jane, I do, but I don't think I'm what she's looking for. I haven't sung since school. Yes, I had an alright voice then, but times have changed. Jane had already asked me, and I told her that I couldn't see how I could commit to the choir and my job."

"She told me that would be your excuse, but doesn't mind if you have to work and miss some rehearsals. But she needs you desperately. Please do this for me. I will owe you big time. Please."

"I am a soft touch." I rolled my eyes. "I'll give it a go, but I'm doing this under protest."

"I know, and I appreciate it. Come on, drink up, it's your round."

"Trust you! I didn't think your generosity would last for long. I shouldn't have said anything to see how many drinks I could get out of you."

"Three was the limit, don't you worry. I'm not that much of a pushover."

"Especially when it involves putting your hand in your pocket."

"Now go and get the drinks in and then you can tell me about your next race?"

"Okay, one more then I am going."

Chapter 2

Dawn

Thursday rolled by. I finished working at five o'clock, so by the time Debbie came round to pick me up for choir practice, I was ready for her. I boiled some potatoes and cooked some salmon for us to have with salad for our dinner. I didn't think I could stomach anything heavy, as the butterflies flying around my stomach were already making me feel sick. Every hour, I had thought of cancelling, but I knew that deep down I would regret it. Debbie was right. I needed to get out and get on with my life. This condition couldn't take away all of me. This was the first step in doing that. At least I would know most of the people at choir. We were, after all, only a small village.

With dinner finished and the dishes put away, Debbie drove me to the community centre. Having spent a couple of minutes looking at the map of the building to find the right room, I looked over towards a door to see a sign saying 'Choir Practice' with a huge black arrow pointing left.

The community centre was a bit of a rabbit warren. The entranceway was lined with concrete tiles, and the walls were painted an odd yellow colour that was neither bright nor dark. Continuing along the corridor, there were branches of corridors with doors off to the right-hand side, and on the left-hand side there was another door that led to a courtyard outside and a separate building which housed the big hall. It was in here that the fundraiser had taken place the last time I'd visited the centre. The choir was in room five, and by the time we reached it, I was out of breath … though mainly due to the sheer anxiety of going out. As soon as we went in, I realised I had nothing to worry about, as the only person there was Jane. Walking towards Debbie and me, she smiled and pulled me in for a hug before moving on to Debbie.

"I am so glad you came. Come and have a seat. As you can see, no one else is here yet."

"Thank you."

Jane turned round to Debbie. "When I spoke to Dawn the other day, she said you weren't stopping by. What a shame," she added with a hint of sarcasm in her voice.

"Oh ha ha," Debbie replied sarcastically. "Am I ever going to live that down? Just let me know if you have any enemies – I am, after all, a secret weapon."

The three of us chuckled.

"Did you want me to drop her off to save you coming back for her?" Jane offered. "If that's all right with both of you, it's no problem for me."

"I think that would be a good idea," I said before Debbie got a chance to reply. "That way, Debbie, you can go home and just put your feet up without worrying about coming back out for me."

A bit flustered, Debbie said, "Okay …thanks for taking her home. But if there are any problems, please give me a ring."

"I will. Now, go home and relax," I demanded. "I will text you later when I get home. Thank you for bringing me. I love you."

"I love you, too. Enjoy yourself."

With that, Debbie left. Just as Jane and I started going through the music, I heard someone say, "Knock knock."

We both turned round to see someone I hadn't seen for a long time, and he had certainly changed. Gone was the slightly tubby, acne-riddled boy, and in his place a real man with muscles in all the right places, confidence pouring out of him. But he still carried his cheekiness, which was easy to see when he turned to Jane and said, "Okay, I gave in, but it was a low blow sending James after me."

"I was desperate! You have no idea how much persuasion that took to get him to twist your arm. I had to agree to name my first child after him!" She rolled her eyes as she turned back to me. "You remember Dawn, don't you, Connor?"

"I certainly do. I haven't seen you around much. How are you?"

"I'm okay," I lied. "You've certainly changed since I last saw you."

"For the better, I hope."

"Of course, although not that there was anything wrong with the old version ..."

"That was a quick save there. You nearly hurt my ego." He gave a sly smile.

"Well, I wouldn't want that."

"Where is that troublemaker sister of yours?"

"Debbie acknowledges that singing isn't, uh, quite her skill."

"Thank heavens for that. I still remember her audition for Grease when we were at school."

"I think everyone does." To which there were more than three people laughing. Only then did I realise that there weren't just the three of us in the room anymore. More people from the village had joined us, all of whom I recognised - one of the perks of living in a small village. You know everyone, at least by sight. It was nice to see people that I felt comfortable with. That was one of the difficulties I'd found going to the conference the previous week - meeting new people and making conversations. People don't realise how much energy it takes to talk to strangers and to think about what to say. That was one of the reasons I had been so tired when I'd got home.

Once everyone had started to settle down, Jane started, and I was surprised at how easy I found it. We had a laugh when people made mistakes, but it was all harmless fun and a great way to relax. Even Connor looked like he was having as much fun as everyone else. Jane even managed to find a way to check that I was okay and that I didn't need a break. As she had said when she'd come to my house, some people decided that some songs weren't for them, so they just sat them out and listened to everyone else. That allowed me to take a break whenever I needed one without standing out, but I was enjoying myself too much for that to happen. It wasn't long before it was time to leave, and after we locked up, we went to Jane's car, where quite a few of the choir members were lingering. There were only a few cars left in the car park. Although we were the last to leave the building, the centre had really good security lights, so it wasn't dark and gloomy and there were still a few people standing round talking before they went their separate ways.

Sitting in her car, we'd begun talking about how the evening had gone when Jane turned the key. But her car wouldn't start.

"No. Come on. Don't do this to me now!"

"Uh, Jane, I'm not sure that shouting at it is going to help. I might not be a mechanic, but it sounds like flat battery."

Just as she was about to answer, there was a knock on the driver's window, and both Jane and I screamed, then we both looked at each other and laughed as we turned and saw Connor through the glass.

Winding down her window, Jane asked, "Are you okay?"

"I apologise for scaring you, but I noticed that you haven't left yet and I wanted to check that you were okay?"

"My car won't start. I think the battery is dead."

"Ah, I don't have any jump leads in my car. I can offer you ladies a lift home or wait until someone else can come? I didn't want to leave you here. It wouldn't be the gentlemanly thing to do. Jane, have you let David know?"

"I was just about to." She held up her phone. "He's working at the restaurant tonight so should be finishing up around now. If I ring him, if it's alright with Dawn, can she sit in your car where it will be warmer?" Jane looked at me to make sure I was okay with what she had said.

"That's okay by me," I replied.

"Of course."

Connor came round to my door and opened it like a gentleman, and he gave me his hand to help me up.

"Right this way, madam," he said as if he was a chauffeur, a cheeky glint in his eye.

I laughed shyly. "Thank you. I appreciate it."

"Anytime. I will put the heating on, then pop back and see what Jane has sorted."

"Thank you."

I watched him in the passenger wing mirror talking to Jane, who then passed her phone to Connor so that he could speak to whoever was on the other end. I presumed it was David. I managed to see her rolling her eyes and laughed to myself, presuming that David was being over-protective.

Jane and Connor came back to the car as Jane got in the back and Connor got in the driver's side.

"I am sorry, Dawn," Jane said. "Connor has offered to give you a lift home and me a lift to David's restaurant."

"It can't be helped, don't worry, and I don't mind ringing Debbie. She did say to let her know if there were any problems."

"Not necessary, this is just a minor hiccup. We can drop

off Jane first and then I will take you home as it's on my way, is that all right?"

"I just don't want to put anyone out."

"You're not putting anyone out. I get the company of two beautiful ladies. I will be the talk of the village!"

Jane laughed. "I'm just glad I let David know before the gossip reached his ears!" We all laughed thinking about what the rumour mill might come up with.

It didn't take long to drop Jane off at the restaurant and get to my house.

"Thank you for the lift Connor, I really appreciate it. Did you want to come in for a drink?"

"No problem. I would love to, but I promised mum I would pop in and see Lily before I went home after choir practice as she had something I needed to pick up for her and I don't want to be too late."

"Okay. Thank you again, and I will see you soon."

With that, I left the car and went to my front door. I turned around and waved goodbye to him as soon as I'd put the key in the lock. I was a bit disappointed about that, as it would have been nice to catch up with him, but also glad because it meant that I could go straight to bed. My body was starting to flag. The night had gone better than I'd expected. I'd thought that I would be more of a hindrance than anything else, but it was the opposite. I couldn't wait for next week's rehearsal. I quickly texted Debbie to thank her for making me go and for arranging it. I then went to bed. Just as I plugged my phone in, I got a text back saying, "You're welcome."

Connor

I can honestly say I wasn't looking forward to being in the choir, but I have to say, it was a laugh and was certainly nowhere near as bad as I'd thought it would be. I'd thought it would be full of my old teachers and friends of my parents and that I would feel like I was out of place, but instead, there was a mix of villagers from all different ages. I was surprised to see Dawn there. I hadn't seen her properly since we'd both left school at eighteen. She'd gone to university and I'd gone to join the police force. Although I'd continued living in the village, I was stationed at Helmslade, the nearest town, and it took me an hour to get to work. It had always been my goal to come back and work from Greengrove Police Station, which was what I had achieved a year ago after my promotion to an inspector. Tonight had put me back into the heart of the village and helped me connect with people I hadn't seen for a long time, and in all honesty, the actual singing wasn't so bad. Maybe I didn't hate James for getting me to go as much as I had thought I would! But I wouldn't tell him that, as I still planned on paying him back for it, as all good friends should.

At least I got the opportunity to be the white knight and drive Jane and Dawn home after Jane's car wouldn't start. I was surprised that Dawn was there on her own. I normally saw her out with her sister; I don't think I'd ever seen her on her own before. Even at school she'd always hung around with Jane, Debbie, Bethany, and Sarah. Jane, Bethany, Debbie, and Dawn were really nice, but unfortunately, Sarah was a really bad piece of work. She bullied everyone, including my friend James's fiancée Lacy. I think that the reason they'd hung around with Sarah, especially when they were younger, was because they were frightened of her. James did tell me that something had happened between the five of them and Sarah was left out on their own, but as I had been in the midst of inspector exams, it was hard to keep up with the gossip. I could never work out why the three of them had hung around with Sarah, especially as they got older, as they were always the nicest people you could meet. Sarah certainly didn't improve with age; in fact, she got worse.

On the drive to drop Dawn off, she kept saying, "Thank you so much."

In the end, I said to her, "I don't want to hear anymore thank yous. It is my pleasure; I was just glad I was there to help."

It was as if she didn't expect people to help her. Living in the village for all my life, and the gossip being better than a local newspaper, everyone tended to know where everyone lived. It's one of the things I loved about living in a village, but it also meant I didn't need direction to her house, which was in one of the newer developments of the village. I think they were built in 1970, which, for the village, was quite new.

Dawn

In the morning I had a text from Debbie asking me how I was after going out the previous night. I replied that I was a bit tired but that I'd tried not to overdo things. Five minutes later, my front door opened, and Debbie shouted that she had arrived. Sitting up just as Debbie sat herself on the empty side of my king size bed, moving the hair out of my eyes, I looked at her and said:

"Debbie, you do know it's 7.00 in the morning?"

"Yes I know, but I need to know what happened last night, and I have to go to work this morning, so I thought I would pop in here first just to make sure you were okay."

"It went well, I didn't overdo it, and Jane, true to her word, didn't make a big thing about checking I was okay. In all honesty, I actually enjoyed myself, and this morning I'm not feeling many ill effects from being out. I know I texted you last night, but thank you for persuading me to go. It was the push I needed."

"You're welcome. Who was there? I bet it was mostly filled with the old choir."

"Actually, it wasn't, and Jane runs it totally different to how the old choir was run; it's more of a fun thing now, although I am sure she is lulling us into a false sense of security! Because it is only quite young, we were singing various genres of songs. A few of our school friends' parents were there, as well as Rebecca, who works with Jane's David, and Connor was there as well."

"Wait, Connor from school?"

"Yes, in fact, he gave me and Jane a lift home as her car wouldn't start. I think James talked him into joining."

"What happened to Jane's car? Why didn't you ring me?"

"I was going to ring you, but Connor said not to disturb you when there was no point, as he could drop us off in the same amount of time it would take you to come and get us."

"Okay, that's fair, and probably very true. So how is Connor? I haven't seen him in ages! I know he came back to work at the police station after his promotion, but as I tend not to get into trouble, I don't get to see him around. I bet he looks better now than he did when he was in Grease. Boy, could he sing."

"It was him!" I announced a bit too loudly.

"What do you mean?"

"When Jane was here the other day, we were talking about the audition you did for a part in Grease so that you could kiss the main lead, but we couldn't remember who it was. It was Connor, wasn't it?"

"I don't know what you are talking about …" she replied, blushing bright red.

"Yes you do. Come on, admit it, it was Connor, wasn't it?"

"Okay, yes, it was Connor. Are you happy now? That was the worst experience of my life."

"Not just your life; it also affected everyone who heard you."

"Oh come on, it wasn't that bad."

"Erm, yes it was. Mr Spencer went off sick with hearing problems the day after your audition."

Rocking into the side of me, Debbie smiled at me.

"I know, but he deserved it. No one liked Mr Spencer, especially after he put us all into detention on a regular basis. Who knew I would be class 10b's secret weapon?"

"That is so true!"

"You know, I like the fact that you can joke again. It's like part of my sister is back." She looked back up at me and nodded firmly. "Now, I love you, but I have to go to work."

"Okay, love you too, see you tomorrow."

I needed to get working, too. I had a few remote meetings during the day, which was unusual for a Friday, but I was glad for them because at least it would break up the monotony of just inputting data and sending emails. At least I'd get to see people as well.

Connor

My shift started at seven o'clock in the morning, and I was due to finish at four o'clock in the afternoon. Firstly I had the daily handover meeting. During the handover meeting the Inspector that worked the nightshift and I talked about some of the reports that were left over from the night that hadn't been completed. I started on the paperwork that had been left over from the night shift; most of it was things to chase up. Luckily, being back in Greengrove, I knew most of the people and where all the secret hangouts were; the places where the teenagers liked to think the adults didn't know existed. But what they didn't realise was that adults had been their age once and at some point those secret places had belonged to them, too. I was just getting ready to go out and talk to a couple who had reported some vandalism when Alan, who used to be the old inspector, whose promotion gave me a job in the village I loved, stopped by my office.

"Knock knock."

"Hey Alan, how are you?"

"I hear someone was out last night singing away?"

"James talked me into it. I thought I would have seen you there. You were part of the old choir, weren't you?"

"I was, and so was your mum. I was thinking about going, but with my promotion, I was worried that I wouldn't be able to commit to it as much as Jane would need me to."

"I was worried about that too, and I tried to use that as an excuse not to get involved, but that was soon cast aside, and last night I understood why. The way Jane runs the choir is completely different from before. It's less formal and 'trying to be the best'. It's relaxed and about having fun and enjoying ourselves. Although, she did say that if the right competition came along and people wanted to do it, then we could enter, but she wants the majority to rule. She did say she wanted to put on a few performances at the community centre, but she wanted to wait until people were comfortable with the new format."

"That sounds much better. I didn't like all the competitions, and when I had to work late, the old choir master really wasn't happy. I might have a word with Jane at May's barbeque tomorrow and see what she says."

"I think that's a great idea. We can also ask mum if she wants to re-join as well." I stood up from my chair and grabbed my jacket from the hook on the wall.

"Are you off out?" Alan asked.

"I have a few people to see following on from last night's shift."

"Problems?"

"Not really. There was some vandalism in the park last night. I have checked the CCTV and it appears to be around six different people, but the witnesses are saying that they weren't local to the village, so I'm going to take a look, have a chat with the witnesses, and see what else turns up."

"Good idea. Let me know if you need any help."

"Will do."

I owed a lot to Alan, as he was the person I'd turned to when I'd decided I wanted follow in my dad's footsteps and join the police force. He'd mentored me throughout my career, helping me with my exams, and he was the first person to congratulate me each time I'd passed and gained promotions.

Both he and my dad had joined the force at the same time, and he had been with my dad when he'd died of a heart attack. They had been chasing a suspect of an armed robbery. Alan was the one who'd held my mum when he'd broke the news, and he was the one I'd turned to whenever I'd had a problem growing up and didn't want to talk to my mum. Throughout my childhood, Alan had always been around. Every Sunday, he would come for lunch as long as he wasn't on duty, and he would pop in and see mum whenever he was out and about. I don't think she would have survived without him, especially in the early years after losing my dad.

Due to the village not being very big, and since it was a sunny day, I decided to walk to my appointments, which gave me the opportunity to stop off at all the secret (not-so-secret) places to see who was around and find out what they knew about the vandalism.

Looking around behind the newsagents where the trees and the grass had overgrown, there was an opening in the fence that had been there for years. Walking through there, I could hear voices.

"Hey guys, it's me, Connor. Can I have a word with you?" I shouted in the hopes that they wouldn't be alarmed when I appeared. Walking to a shed, I saw a couple of the older boys from the village, one of which was Debbie and Dawn's cousin, Adam, and the other his friend Dominic.

"Hey, Connor, what are you doing here?" Adam asked, looking worried. Adam and Dominic were quiet teenagers; they were never normally in any bother. Dominic's brother was well known in the police station, but Dominic certainly didn't follow his example.

"Hey guys, I know it wasn't either of you, but do you know anything about the vandalism in the park last night? Did you see or hear anything?"

"Umm … no, I don't know anything," Adam said. "But I have college this afternoon, so I can keep my ears open. I saw the park this morning on my way here; someone's made a right mess of it. I don't understand why someone would want to do that to a kid's playground. The amount of broken glass around is so dangerous. My little sister plays there, so it needs to be safe."

"Thanks, Adam. If you could listen out, that would

be great. I know there were some of the community centre members clearing up when I walked past, and I had a quick conversation with Lily, from the Community Centre, and she said they are going to put a working team together to repaint the equipment."

"That's great; I'll have a word with Lily and see if I can help. Can I count on you, Dom?" Adam asked his quiet friend.

Dominic shrugged in response.

"Thanks, boys. I'll catch you later, but let me know if you hear anything."

I then went to interview some of the witnesses. I loved this part of the job, walking around the village and talking to people.

It was nearing the end of my shift by the time I got back to the station. The handover was quick, as there wasn't much to report, and that was normally what Greengrove was like.

I had arranged with Mum that I would stop in and have dinner with her tonight, and if she was up to it, I'd suggested going to the pub owned by my friend, James, although these days, he only tended to work during the day as he had hired a pub manager. Using my key to open Mum's front door, I shouted, "Hi Mum, it's me."

"Hi, love, I'm in the living room." I knew from her voice that the pub wasn't happening.

Moving into the living room, I saw her sitting on her chair. Leaning down to kiss her on the cheek, I could tell she wasn't having a great day before I even asked the question: "How are you feeling today?"

"I am exhausted, and the pain is really strong today. I have tried my tens machine but that isn't even taking the edge off today. Is it alright if we don't go out for dinner tonight?"

"Of course it is. I think we should get a takeaway instead. Do you want Indian or Chinese?"

"I won't eat much, so you choose. If we have Chinese, I'll have a soup, and if we have Indian, I'll just have a starter."

"Indian it is. I'll call the restaurant. What would you like?"

"Umm, chicken tikka starter."

"No problem."

Popping into the kitchen to make a cup of tea for mum while I ordered dinner, I saw that the kitchen wasn't in its normal tidy state; in fact, the sink was full of mugs and what were obviously Mum's lunch plates for the last couple of days. Due to the fact that there was still food left on the plates, it was obvious she hadn't eaten much either. The workbenches needed a wipe over, and Mum had loaded the washing machine but hadn't put it on. I quickly set about putting the kitchen to rights. It was obvious that Mum was having a flare-up, but instead of telling me, she'd tried to cope through it. As soon as her drink was ready and the kitchen looked a bit better with the washing machine and dishwasher running, I went into the living room, carrying the mugs.

"Here you are, mum. Tea is ready and dinner will be about half an hour."

I sat opposite her at the table and looked her square in the eyes. "How long have you been struggling with your flare-up?"

She averted my gaze, then sighed in defeat. "I was okay yesterday. I was just a bit fatigued. But the pain started last night as I tried to get to sleep, so I tried the heated blanket that you got me, and that helped a little bit, but I didn't get much sleep. Then this morning, the pain was just as severe. You would have thought, after all these years of having fibromyalgia, that I would know what to do and how to help a flare-up, but it always seems that each one is as individual as the last."

"Mum, you weren't okay yesterday. I saw the kitchen. I would say that it's been at least three days since you've been okay. When you got worse, why didn't you send me a message?

I would have popped in or asked one of your friends to pop in and help, especially around lunchtime."

"I didn't want to worry you, and I knew you would be coming round tonight, so I thought I would be alright coping till then. I spent most of the day asleep under my blanket anyway."

"I don't want you to struggle, Mum, and neither do your friends. I could have asked May or Lily to help you. I bet you didn't even ring them to let them know that you weren't feeling well. And what about Alan? Didn't you speak to him last night?"

"I just thought I was tired, so I didn't say anything. He does so much, and I didn't want to bother May or Lily either. I don't want to be a burden to anyone."

"I know you don't, Mum, but you know as well as I do that every so often you need to ask for help. I know it's difficult, but please ask for help. I don't like seeing you like this, and you know anyone would help you."

"I know. I'm sorry." She glared at me as if to say 'This conversation is over'. I rolled my eyes but smiled in spite of myself. "Now that I have had the lecture …" she continued, "tell me how choir went. Did you enjoy yourself?"

I knew she hadn't been out the house that day, and if

she had been holed up at home feeling sick and hiding from people, then she wouldn't have heard the gossip from last night, and trust me, in this village, there was always gossip. Some of it could be quite funny when stories were twisted and turned to make them more dramatic than reality. I knew anything I told her would be closer to the truth than anything she would hear on the streets.

"It was okay. Jane has really got a good mix of people going. It's not like the old choir, it's much more laid back, and the variety of songs we sang seems to appeal to everyone. I wasn't the only one who was there for the first time; one of the Simpson twins was there as well."

"Oh, please tell me it wasn't Debbie! Her singing is famous for all the wrong reasons."

"Luckily, it was Dawn. Debbie just dropped her off."

"I haven't seen Dawn around the village for ages. She is a lovely girl, although both of them are and should never have been caught up with that awful Sarah. To be honest, none of them should have done, but I think Debbie, Dawn, Bethany and Jane felt stuck in that situation until they were strong enough and old enough to fight her. Thank God Sarah has left."

I nodded in agreement. Just then the doorbell went; our dinner had arrived. I didn't realise that the forty minutes that they had quoted for delivery had passed. Mum was just about to get up to answer it when I said, "Don't worry, I've got this; you just sit there and rest."

"You are a good boy, you know."

"I know," I chuckled and went to the door to retrieve dinner.

"Only a small amount for me," I heard from the living room.

"Just relax, I know what I'm doing."

She left me alone to dish up and bring it through to her on passing her dish.

"Thank you, son. Now, tell me more about last night."

Sitting down with a bowl of curry in my lap, I said, "I don't want this getting back to James, because he thinks he owes me a really large favour, but ... I enjoyed myself last night. It was fun catching up with everyone I hadn't seen that much of since I was stationed in Hambleton. I've been busy adjusting to my promotion and taking over from Alan and his big shoes. Other than meeting up with James occasionally, I haven't had time to catch up with anyone else."

"I'm glad, and your secret is safe with me. I won't say a word to James." She smiled.

"It was nice to feel part of the community again. I hung around till Jane had locked up, and while I was waiting for Dawn and Jane to leave I realised there was something wrong with Jane's car. The battery was dead, so I gave her a lift to David's restaurant and Dawn a lift home."

"I am glad. I know you missed Greengrove when you weren't here. It's nice to know I have brought up a knight in shining armour. I wish I had got out into the village. I wonder what the gossip would have been about your good deed. I think we need to encourage Alan to join the choir. It would be nice for him to get out again."

"I dread to think what the gossip would have been this morning, although I talked to Alan about the choir today when he came to my office, and I think he is seriously considering it. He said you used to go as well, so maybe you should consider it?" Mum looked at me sceptically, so I changed the subject. "Do you think you will be well enough for May's community barbeque tomorrow?"

"I hope so. I would like to go if I can."

"Do you want me to pick you up?"

"No, it's alright. Alan offered to do it when I spoke to him yesterday."

"Alright, but if you need me, then let me know."

Mum didn't eat much of her dinner, only eating two of the five pieces that you got as it was only a starter portion to start with, so as soon as I had finished my curry I picked her plate off the coffee table and I said to her, "I'm going to put the leftovers away and then clean the dishes. Do you want me to make you a bedtime chocolate while I am in there?"

"Ooh, that would be lovely. I wonder if you could help me go to bed as well? I think the stairs might be a bit much today on my own."

"Give me ten minutes and I will help you."

"You'd better take those leftovers home because I don't think I'll get round to eating them."

"Okay, will do, as long as you're sure, but I am going to let your friends know you haven't been well."

Half an hour later and Mum was tucked up into her bed, so I left to go back to my place. I texted Alan, Lily, and May to say that Mum was having a flare-up. Alan was not best pleased that he didn't know and phoned me back straight away to make sure there was nothing he needed to do, but I think he planned on having his own talk with Mum before the barbeque tomorrow. Sometimes Mum was a bit too stubborn for her own good.

Dawn

It was just after ten o'clock Saturday morning when Debbie came to pick me up to go shopping after a quick trip to the coffee shop, where we had a toasted sandwich and a drink. The trip round the supermarket really did me in. I left Debbie paying and packing while I sat down on one of the seats that they had near the checkout so that I could have a little rest.

I sat next to an elderly man who said, pointing to my sister, "A young thing like you should be over there helping her pack. It would help cut down on the queues if there was two of you packing."

I was taken aback. I could feel myself get really tense, and I am sure I was bright red I was so embarrassed. I know I was sitting ramrod straight because I could feel the pain it was causing in my back, but I didn't want to get into an argument, so I just replied, "Oh I would love to, but I have just been released from hospital and I'm not allowed to lift anything." With that, I got up to join Debbie, who was nearly done. A little way down the road Debbie said to me, "Okay, what happened? You have been really tense and angry and upset since we left the supermarket."

"It's nothing, really!"

"It obviously is, because you are so wound up it is transferring to me. So, come on, sis, spill."

"Alright, when I was sitting down the old man told me that I should have been helping you instead of sitting there because it would help get the queues down."

"Are you kidding me? Who did he think he was?"

"It's okay. I told him I was just out of hospital and not allowed to lift anything."

"You didn't need to tell him anything, you had every right to sit there, you should have told me I would have said something to him!"

"I know, that's why I didn't. I just wanted to get out of there!"

"You're to ignore him, he is just a stupid ignorant man!"

"I know!"

As the supermarket was about half an hour away from the village, we didn't get back to my house until two o'clock. Debbie helped me put away the shopping, then we sat and had a cup of tea.

"Are you coming to the community barbeque at May's house this afternoon?"

"I was going to, but I'm not sure now. I know I haven't been in a long time, and it was nice seeing everyone the other day…"

"You're still thinking about that stupid man and his nasty comment. Put him behind you. No one like that will be at the barbeque, I promise. Earlier on, you were thinking about going, and I was so glad you were thinking about the positives of getting out and about. Don't let an idiot spoil that. I tell you what, why don't you sit and rest for a little while and I can do a few jobs for you, then we will leave around 4.30. How does that sound?"

"I don't want you to come here and think that you need to do jobs all the time."

"It's honestly not a problem. I just thought I would help hoover and then you can spend more of your energy spoons at May's barbeque. I win out of this scenario because I get my sister back."

I looked her in the eye. "Thank you, Debs. I know I have said it before, but I don't know what I would do without you."

"Let's hope you never find out." With a smile, she left me in the living room to go and get the hoover and prove to me she was the best sister I could ever have.

We drove to May's, but as we expected, there was nowhere to park, so Debbie dropped me off and went to search for a space. As I was waiting for her, Connor's mum, Charlotte, and Alan, who was now the village's chief inspector, came walking towards me.

Charlotte was walking with a walking stick in her left hand and Alan was supporting her on her right hand side. I knew Charlotte had always had health problems since Connor had been at school.

"Hello, Dawn, long time no see."

"Hello, Charlotte, Alan. How are you both?"

"We're good, thanks, how are you?" Charlotte answered for both of them.

"I'm okay. Busy as always, and still working from home. I'm just waiting for Debbie. She had to find a parking place."

"I think she might be a little way away," Alan said. "I don't think I've ever seen so many cars here!"

We all looked around to see parked cars on both sides of the road, and even some of the driveways of houses had more than one car parked. This afternoon's barbeque certainly seemed to be popular.

"I think the weather has brought everyone out, but the fear of rain clearly made them bring their cars instead of walking," Alan joked.

"Yes, you're probably right," I replied, but no sooner had I got the words out than a burst of pain shot through my leg and hip, and there was nothing I could do to stop the involuntary wince that I wore on my face.

Charlotte put her hand on my arm and asked, "Are okay, Dawn? You look like you are in pain."

"Oh yes, don't worry," I lied. I couldn't bear the idea of anyone thinking me weak. "I think I might have slept badly last night and caught a nerve."

"As long as you are sure. Did you want to go inside and find somewhere to sit to take the pressure off it? I'm sure Debbie will know where you are."

"I think that might be a good idea."

"Are you okay walking on your own, or do you want to borrow my arm?" Alan asked.

"I'll be fine, but thank you for the offer."

Pushing open the front door to May's house, Alan shouted, "May, Mike, anyone there?"

From the distance, we saw Mike pop his head round the kitchen door.

"Hello, Alan! You seem to have your hands full with three lovely ladies." It was at that moment that I realised that Debbie had returned from parking the car.

"I know, I'm a lucky man! Where is everyone? Judging by the parking outside, it seems the whole village is here," Alan replied.

"Come through. Everyone and their wife seems to be outside, and some have even brought food and drink, so we aren't going to run out. James just went to the community centre to borrow some sports equipment for the kids to have a game of football or rounders out on the field."

We followed Alan out through the living room to the double doors that led to the back garden and patio area. I couldn't believe how many people were outside. It had been quite a while since I'd been to one of May's barbeques, but I didn't remember it ever being so busy.

Coming up on my left-hand side, Debbie whispered to me, "Were you alright? I didn't mean to be so long."

"Don't worry, I was fine. I just had a moment where pain shot up my leg, but it's gone now. I just think it might be best if I sit down for a little while."

Looking around for a chair, Charlotte beckoned me over to sit on the seat next to her.

"Why don't you rest your leg for a little while? I haven't seen you for ages."

"Thank you, Charlotte."

I had been sitting there for about half an hour when Mike shouted, "Grub's up!" All at once, there were three queues of people at each beautifully-laid-out table. One had cold salads and breads, another had the hot barbequed food, and the last one had the cakes and cheese and biscuits. It didn't take long for the queues to go down, and just as I was about to ask Charlotte if she wanted me to get her any food, Alan came up and gave her a full plate.

Debbie was just walking by with Jane and Lacy when she suggested that we all get food together. In pairs, the four of us walked towards the tables, and I talked to Lacy:

"Do you have lots of events coming up?"

"Not really, Lorraine is taking the bulk of them so that I can concentrate on Jane's wedding."

"Is she a bridezilla?"

"No comment,"

"I heard that," Jane said from behind us, and we all laughed.

The four of us had moved on a lot since school. I was glad that, over the years, we'd realised we were in the wrong going along with Sarah's bullying, and we had since ditched Sarah. Although I knew that Lacy had forgiven us and put it all behind her, sometimes I still felt guilty and ashamed of what we had been part of.

Getting a little bit of food, we all decided to sit and eat our dinner on the grass. Just as we were about to sit down, James, David, and Connor appeared carrying three blankets between them.

"Careful, ladies. Before you sit down, let us put the blankets down for you," James said before leaning over and giving Lacy a kiss. With the blankets laid out, the men helped us all sit down by holding our plates so that we could get comfy before passing the plates back to us, although I did notice both David and James steal some food before handing the plates back. The men then went off to get their own food before they joined us.

The seven of us all sat around on the blanket until it got to nine o'clock. Talking and laughing around with friends really did make the time go by quickly. Connor was the first to get up from the blanket as he went to say goodbye to his mum and make sure she didn't need anything. I was watching Connor as he spoke to his mum. He really treated her as if she was a queen; he helped her up off the chair and made sure she had everything she needed before he lent her his hand as he helped her get through the front of the house while Alan brought the car through. Nothing seemed to be too much trouble for him as far as his mother was concerned. Even when she sat in the car and he walked away, he looked back to make sure she was alright.

With the party breaking up, Debbie helped me get off the rug as my legs and back had seized up, and she didn't let go of me until I could feel everything again.

"I'm going to see if Mike and May need any help, but if they don't, I'll go and bring the car round. Will you be alright here for a little bit?"

"Of course, I'll be fine. I might try to walk around to loosen my body a bit," I replied.

While I was walking around with a bin bag, collecting the rubbish off the tables, Connor walked over.

"Hey, are you okay?"

"Oh yes, although help is always appreciated."

Working together, we cleared all the tables, and behind us, James and David were folding them up ready to go. In no time, the garden was cleared, and although I was starting to get tired, I was happy I had achieved something that day. I turned to thank Connor for his help just as my phone buzzed. My smart watch told me Debbie had texted and she had found a place to stop outside and that she was waiting for me.

"Uh, thanks for your help, guys," I said quietly. "I've got to go. Debbie's waiting."

Connor turned as smiled at me. "You're welcome – I'll

walk you to your car." I gratefully accepted as he offered his arm.

"I wondered if you are going to choir on Thursday and whether you would like me to pick you up to save Debbie dropping you off?" Connor asked. "I will even drive you home, as well."

"That would be great, as long as you don't mind?"

"Of course I don't mind. I wouldn't have asked if I did."

"That would be wonderful. In fact, why don't you come early and we can have some dinner before we go?"

"That would be great." He smiled, a twinkle in his eye. "See you Thursday. Shall I come around 5.30 after work?"

"That would be great."

Getting to Debbie's car, Connor held the door open while I got in.

"See you after work on Thursday then, Dawn. Bye, Debbie."

He closed the car door and tapped the top of the roof, and Debbie pulled away. That was when the teasing started.

"So come on then, why is Connor seeing you after work?"

"We are having dinner before choir, as he offered to take

me to save you the job."

"That will be nice. You never told me he had bulked out and become all muscly."

"I didn't notice."

"What do you mean you didn't notice? You're not blind. You know anyone can see that Connor is all man."

"I don't really think I am in a position to look, do you?"

"Why not?"

"Oh, come off it, Debs. What would I have to offer someone like Connor?"

"Don't start with the pity party." She frowned at me. "Yes, you have a condition which affects your life, but please don't let it take your hopes away that somewhere out there is a man willing to walk through the highs and lows of your condition with you. And I think Connor is that man. He knows what it's like to live with someone with a lifelong medical condition; he was still at school when his mum first became ill, and at that time, he became her carer."

"I don't think he is interested in a relationship with me. I think he was just being friendly." I sighed. "Can we not talk about this anymore? I don't want the pressure of thinking this is something that it's not. Please."

On the drive home as I looked out the window I thought about what Debbie had said about his mum having a condition and Connor looking after her and what I'd witnessed at the barbeque.

Debbie pulled up to my drive and said, "Will you be alright, or do you want me to help you inside?"

"I'll be fine," I snapped, then instantly regretted it. "Thank you for taking me. I had a wonderful time."

"Anytime. I'll phone you tomorrow evening, but if you need anything, don't hesitate to call me. Love you."

"Love you too."

I walked three steps towards the house, and the next thing I knew, I was lying on the front grass. Trying to get up, I saw Debbie come running.

"Oh Dawn, what happened? Are you okay? Can you get up or do you want me to phone for an ambulance?"

"I'm fine. There's no need to panic, and no, I don't need an ambulance … but can you help me get up?"

I pulled at her hands as she helped me get up. There were so many emotions running through me. I was mad at myself for being so useless that I couldn't even walk a few steps without even falling down, then I was furious at myself for that ridiculous thought. Anyone can fall down at anytime. I was embarrassed that I had literally faceplanted on the floor. I was glad it was in front of Debbie and not anyone else. And lastly, I was exhausted both mentally and physically. I don't even know how I managed to continue the walk into house. I just wanted to lie there and cry. There were times when I just hated being me.

"It's lucky you landed on the grass. I think that softened the fall."

"I think my right foot just didn't fancy lifting up properly and thought it would give the grass a hug."

"Come on, I'll help you get inside."

"Thanks."

Although stiff and a bit shook up, I had managed to get away without a graze or serious damage.

"I tell you what, why don't I help you to your room? You can get ready for bed and I will bring up a drink and the heat pad. Hopefully that will help with the stiffness. What do you think?"

"That sounds great, thank you."

"Stop saying 'thank you'. Now come on, let's get you upstairs."

Once I was settled in bed, I took two paracetamol in the hopes that would stop any pain on the way and quickly fell asleep. I didn't even remember Debbie leaving.

The next morning, I woke up stiff and sore. There were a few bruises on my side, but otherwise, as nothing was broken, I would say I got off quite lightly. Although it was slow progress, I managed to get a few things marked off my to do list and prepared myself some of the leftovers May had given everyone to take home. At least they hadn't gotten damaged in the fall, and it meant that I didn't need to cook. That would have been one thing too many today. As promised, Debbie phoned to see how I was, but other than that, it was a quiet day, which was what I needed after the last few days. I spent most of the day just resting on the sofa and reading my book under my favourite blanket.

Chapter 3

Connor

I was chuffed at my idea of asking Dawn if she wanted me to take her to choir on Thursday. I was going to have to drive past her house to get to choir anyway, and there was no point her sister going out of her way. But most of all, it allowed me to spend some time with her, talk to the real Dawn and not the one who hid behind her outspoken sister. On Sunday I took part in a bike ride in Helmslade, although they weren't my favourite things to do; I felt that they were just another different type of training for my triathlons.

At work, things were just ticking over. I hadn't realised how much paperwork was involved in being an inspector, although I had an inkling Alan might have pushed some my way to prepare me for the next step towards promotion. If paperwork was my future, I wasn't sure I even wanted to be promoted. It was too early to tell, anyway. I hadn't even been an inspector for two years yet.

I did stop by his office on Monday to check in and find out how Mum was after the barbeque. Although I'd phoned her to check, she sometimes wouldn't let on how difficult life could be. But Alan reassured me that she was feeling much better than she had been on Friday and had told her off again for not saying anything. She hated feeling like she was a burden.

With a busy life, just as I liked it, Thursday came quickly, and I was looking forward to seeing Dawn. As always in this village, it didn't take long to drive to her house. In fact, it took longer walking from my car to her front door because I was stopped by both of her neighbours asking questions.

"Have you caught the vandals yet?"

"The play park didn't deserve such destruction."

"How is Dawn involved with the play park debacle?"

"Surely Dawn isn't a suspect? She's so quiet and friendly. She would never do anything illegal."

I replied with a cheeky grin, "Ah, it's always the ones you don't expect." I laughed at their confused expressions, then took pity on them. Besides, I didn't want anyone badmouthing Dawn. "If you must know, I'm here for dinner, then I'll take her to choir.

"Ah, that makes perfect sense," old Mrs Bridges said (Dawn's neighbour on her right-hand side). "You'd better run along and not keep your date waiting."

Just as I reached Dawn's front door, I heard them both say, "They'd make a wonderful couple."

It didn't take Dawn long to answer the door, and just after saying hello, I saw her wave to her neighbours.

"Please come in. I've just put together a platter of cheese, ham, bread, and pickles. I hope that's okay?"

"Sounds perfect to me." I smiled at her, and as soon as the front door was closed, I said, "According to Mrs Bridges, we make a lovely couple. Your neighbours think we're dating."

Dawn's face went bright red as she stuttered to get the words out. "Oh no, I'm so sorry. That's going to be all round the village quicker than a cold. I really am sorry. I should have thought about that before I invited you here."

"Don't be silly! If they want to decide that I'm dating you, then who am I to stop them? Unless of course you don't want to be seen with me?" I was trying to lighten the mood and take away her embarrassment, but my last comment didn't exactly have the desired effect.

"Oh no, it's not that at all. I mean, look at you, then look at me. If anyone should be embarrassed, it should be you."

"Well, I am looking, and I know I'm not embarrassed, so neither should you be. Now that's sorted, should we eat?"

"Oh yes, I'm sorry." She led me into her living room. "Here, take a seat. Can I get you a drink? I have, water, tea, coffee, various flavours of tea, some lemonade, Coke - I didn't think we should have wine before we go, and I don't drink much, but I do have some wine and some cans of beer if that's better?"

"Calm down, Dawn. There is nothing to be nervous about. We are just two friends having dinner together. Now then, I would love a glass of lemonade." I sighed as she looked at the floor and mumbled another apology under her breath. "I wish I had never told you what your neighbours said, but I wanted you to be warned. If I hadn't told them I was here for dinner, they would have continued to assume you were part of my investigation. Better this than thinking you're a criminal, no?"

Dawn nodded sheepishly.

"I found their comments funny, really."

"You're right, sorry. It is funny thinking you and me would be going out."

With that, she went to go to the kitchen to get our drinks, but I could see in the way her shoulders dropped and her lower energy that she had taken my words the wrong way.

By the time she came back to the living room, the most amazing platter was set out on her coffee table. Her face showed a smile that was obviously fake, as it didn't reach her eyes. The twinkle that was always in her eyes was missing, and I would have done anything to get it back. As she sat by the side of me and passed me a white plate and knife to dish out my choices, I knew I needed to set things right.

"Dawn, I think you took what I said wrong. I didn't mean 'funny' as in me and you being together, I meant 'funny' as in the way this village works and the idea that two people can't have a meal together without the village gossips labelling them as the next great couple."

Dawn's phone buzzed, and as she looked at the screen, she burst out laughing.

"What? What is it?"

"Debbie wants to make sure she will be my maid of honour when we get married, which, according to everyone, will be August." She sighed like a weight had dropped off her shoulders. "I understand what you mean now when you said that the village gossip is funny. You weren't kidding. I guess I just hadn't listened too much to recent gossip to take much notice."

"I think the best piece of gossip I heard was that when Lily had visitors in, someone decided it was because she was leaving the village and running away with a tall boy. I mean, think about it Lily skipping town with a large chest of drawers!

The truth was that she was clearing out the loft and sending her husband's collection of car memorabilia that was up in the loft to auction to raise funds for the community centre."

They both laughed.

"I missed that one! This village's gossip can be worse than being back at school. Come on, we'd better eat, otherwise we will be getting hungry during choir practice."

"Who knows what the gossips would make of our stomachs rumbling at the same time?"

Her sister's text seemed to have put her mind at rest, and the twinkle in her eyes was back as we shared stories about some of the gossip we had heard over the years.

After we had eaten enough, I helped to move everything into the kitchen before we set out to leave the house. As I helped her put her coat on, I noticed that standing by the coat stand was a walking stick. I didn't want to make assumptions as to why she would have one in the house, but I also didn't know how to ask if she needed it. I hadn't seen her use one last week, so I just left it where it was but kept an eye on her just in case.

Walking into the choir room, we both went our separate ways. I walked over to talk to Alan, who had decided to give choir another go, and Dawn walked over to Jane.

"Hey Connor, glad you're here. I hear congratulations are in order. Have you spoken to your mum?"

"Don't you start, Alan. I take it you're offering the congratulations for whatever you heard on the grape vine?"

He chuckled. "Apparently you're getting married in August and expecting your first child in September."

"Wow, they're not even trying to make sense anymore!"

From across the room, I heard Dawn shout, "I am not pregnant! That is so far from being a possibility, you wouldn't believe it."

Everyone turned round to look at her, and as soon as she realised what she had said, her face went bright red and her eyes darted about, trying to find the nearest exit.

Jane was just about to say something when Stephen, who owned the DIY store in the village, said, "Oh don't worry, he's probably waiting for the wedding night like I did with my Doris, although he would have to work miracles for you to get to your due date."

Everyone started laughing at Stephen, and Jane decided that was the time to get organised, thank heavens. As we were moving into our places, I had just enough time to quietly ask Alan to explain to my mum that she didn't need to get her knitting needles out just yet. Obviously, Mum had decided choir wasn't for her.

Maybe she needed a bit more persuading. Mind you, with the way the gossip was going, it was a good job she wasn't there. But I would have to ring her when I got home to put her right on the true story, although she had known that I was going to Dawn's house for dinner, so she'd probably guessed.

Things quietened down while we set about singing in groups. At one point, I looked over to see Dawn, who was beginning to look pale, and then I saw Jane mouth to ask her if she wanted to sit down, to which I saw Dawn respond with a quick nod. It was so quick that, if I hadn't been looking, I wouldn't have noticed it, but as soon as the song finished, I saw Dawn walk over to a seat and take a drink of water from the bottle that she'd brought with her. She sat out the last three songs, and I only got a chance to check on her at the end, by which point some of her colour had returned. I walked over to her, and she smiled up at me.

"Are you okay?" I asked.

"Oh yes, I just didn't think I could reach some of the high notes for those songs," she said, not looking me in the eye.

I knew this was a lie. Not only had I seen Jane's question

to her, but I remembered she had sung those songs before. Something was going on with Dawn.

"I just want to help Jane put the tables and chairs back, then we can get going if you're ready," I said.

"Of course, I'll be ready."

While putting the tables and chairs away with Jane, I thought I would ask her if she would tell me what was wrong with Dawn.

"Can I ask you a question, Jane?"

"Of course."

"Is Dawn alright? I saw you ask her if she wanted to sit down, and before that, she looked really pale."

"As far as I know, she's okay. I don't remember asking her if she wanted to sit down. Are you sure that's what I said?"

I frowned at her with suspicion, but knew I wasn't going to get any more out of her. Once everything had been put away, I escorted Jane and Dawn outside, keeping a close eye on Dawn. I know in my gut there was something wrong with her, and because I cared, I was determined to not give up in my search for the truth, even if it took a while.

On the drive back to Dawn's house we talked about the

choir and Jane's new role as choir master. I said: "Jane is a really good choir master. From what Alan has said, she is much better than the previous one."

"She is. She really enjoys it, and when I talked to her before I joined, she said she wanted it to be relaxed and not competitive, with a mix of music suitable for everyone's tastes, and I think she has achieved that."

"I think she has. What is your favourite kind of music?"

"I really like pop rock, but I can listen to anything really. What about you?"

"It's the same really, it's more about the song than the genre for me."

With that we got to her house. "Thank you for the lift would you like to come in?"

"Not tonight if that's okay. I have an early shift tomorrow, but I will definitely take a rain check. I will see you Thursday when I pick you up if not before."

"Definitely. Thank you, Connor."

Over the next few weeks, we got into a pattern on a Thursday. I would collect her from her house to go to choir practice, before which we would have some dinner. We were slowly getting more comfortable with each other, and although

I was no closer to discovering her secret, I was beginning to look forward to Thursdays so much so that I'd decided to ask her to be my date for Jane and David's wedding in two weeks' time. The thought of asking her made me more nervous than anything else I'd ever done … strangely even more so than the dangerous things I'd done in my police career.

As in previous weeks, a platter was laid out and the lemonade was waiting for me when I got there. To get it out of the way, as soon as we had sat down and filled our plates up, I asked quietly, "I wondered if you had a date for Jane's wedding?"

"I'm sorry, I didn't hear you. What did you say?"

I cleared my throat, thick with nerves, and tried again. "I just … wondered if you had a date for Jane's wedding?"

"Oh no, I was just going to go with Debbie because she hasn't got a date either, and we told Jane we would be each other's plus one. I think Jane was happy about that because it was two people less she needed to sort food for. Why?"

"Well … I wondered if you wanted to go with me."

"Oh!" She paused, then looked at me apologetically. "I would love to … but I promised myself to Debbie, and I don't want to leave her on her own."

"That's no problem. Why don't I take both of you? That would really put the gossips to work. From what I understand, we are all sitting on the same table anyway. I think May called us 'the young ones' when she helped with the table plan. Why don't you ask Debbie? We can either walk or I can drive us there so you can both have a drink."

As soon as I mentioned walking, her face winced in pain, but no sooner had it come than the look was washed away as if it had never happened.

"Thank you, I'll text her and let you know what she says."

And that was how it was left as we continued to finish our dinner and go to choir. It was only on the way home that she told me that Debbie had agreed to go with my suggestion, as long as it was okay, and I reassured her it was.

The next two weeks continued along the same lines. I watched Dawn a few times during choir practice and noticed that a few times she sat out a few songs, and there were always subtle movements between Jane and Dawn as if there was a secret code that no one was privy to. The gossip about me and Dawn had died down, but it took a week longer to do so than I'd thought it would, thanks to DIY Stephen's comment about us waiting till our wedding day.

Dawn

It was the day of Jane's wedding, and Connor was picking Debbie and me up from my house at 1.30 so that we could get to David's restaurant in time for the 2 o'clock wedding. Jane had decided that the wedding of her dreams wouldn't be in a church but in David's restaurant. In a selfish way, I was relieved that the wedding wouldn't move venues, as having to move between two destinations would wear me out more and then I wouldn't be able to enjoy myself. Also, churches tended to be quite cold, and when I got cold, it was hard to warm up again.

Debbie had stayed the night and we were having a lazy morning before getting ready. We were in my bedroom doing my make-up and I was sitting on my dressing table stool as she asked the question I was hoping she wouldn't ask because I was afraid to answer:

"You like Connor, don't you?"

"Of course, he's very nice. Don't you?"

"Don't be obtuse, you know that's not what I meant!"

"Okay, yes, I do like him, but I am frightened to like him."

"What, why?"

"You know why!"

"No, I don't." By this time she had stopped what she was doing and put down the brushes to sit on the floor in her pyjamas and look up at me with a questioning look.

"When I was diagnosed, it was a complete change for me and for you in how my life was going to be. There are a lot of things I won't be able to do that other people our age can do. Connor is into fitness. The man competes in triathlons, for crying out loud; he isn't going to want a girlfriend who sometimes can't even walk up a flight of steps without needing help."

"You're not that person all the time. Your condition is part of you, yes, but it isn't you. You are kind, caring, wonderful, funny and a pleasure to be with and it is that person that Connor, if he is interested in you, will want to be with. The gossip in the village is that he is interested. I think you should tell him about your fibromyalgia and let him decide whether he wants to go out with you or not. And if he doesn't, then he's not the man I thought he was."

"I will think about it."

"Good, now let's get this make-up done, then we can finish getting dressed."

As promised, Debbie didn't put too much make-up

on me. I never normally wear make-up unless it's a special occasion, and I didn't want too much on as I still wanted it to look natural. Looking in the mirror, I was pleased with the results. She had also managed to put my hair up in a half-up half-down where the sections that were used for the half-up were twisted from the front to the back. Debbie went back into the spare room to get into her dress while I went and put my dress on. I decided to put on a long flowy one because I didn't need help getting it on and off as it just fitted over my head. It was also lovely and summery with poppies all over it. I had just put it on when Debbie came into the room looking amazing, wearing a fitted peach dress that stopped just above the knee.

"No offence, sis, but you're not wearing that."

"What's wrong with it?"

"Nothing. If it's a lovely summer's day, it's your go-to dress. I know that you have something much better in your wardrobe for the wedding and you are just taking the easy route out by grabbing the old faithful. Come on, let's get something else on."

Walking over to my wardrobe, Debbie picked out the peach Jersey skater dress I had originally decided to wear.

"What's wrong with this one? I thought you bought this especially."

"I started to worry that it made me look fat."

"Don't be silly. You looked gorgeous in it when you tried it on and I bet you will look the same now, so get the old faithful off and put this one on before Connor gets here."

"Yes, boss."

"You better believe it, and don't forget it," she said as she walked away. After looking back over her shoulder to gave me a wink, she left me to change. To be honest, I did feel better in the skater dress than I had in my old faithful. I should have just stuck with my original plan.

Walking into the living room, Debbie said, "You even walk better in that. You are walking with confidence, standing tall, as if you can take on everything, whereas in the other dress it was as if you had the world on your shoulders, as your body was slumped over as you walked. Does that make sense?"

"It does, and to be honest, you were right. I feel so much better in this one. Thank you. I love you, even if you are bossy."

Connor arrived just before 1.30. I liked that he was always on time. He wasn't one of those people who thought they were so important that they could turn up whenever they wanted to, knowing you would be waiting for them. I remember Debbie going out with someone like that once; his name was Trevor, or 'Terrible Trevor', as we called him. On one of their dates, he was supposed to turn up at seven o'clock, but instead he turned up at ten thirty, by which time Debbie had called me and we'd gone to the pub for dinner. That was when she'd decided enough was enough and if he was so selfish that he didn't realise his behaviour was unacceptable, then he never would. When he turned up, she told him to go away and delete her number.

When I opened the door to Connor, who was wearing a charcoal grey suit, white shirt and a silver tie, he took my breath away. Connor was not one to look scruffy, but this was a different level of smart, and I have to say, I couldn't take my eyes off him. Smiling at me, he said:

"Wow, you look beautiful. I really am going to be the envy of all the men there."

"Thank you." I blushed.

"Are you lovely ladies ready?"

"Yes, we are," called Debbie. "Is there any chance we could drive? These heels are killing me today! But they were the only ones that went with this dress."

I knew she was covering for me because I was worried about walking there and having a full day of socialising then having to walk back.

"Of course, I don't mind at all. I wouldn't like for you to have to ruin that dress with a pair of more practical shoes."

"You are such a good man," she said as she came down the stairs, giving one of her dazzling smiles. "You appreciate the trouble we go to trying to make things match. Now, show us to our carriage," she demanded before walking out the door, leaving both Connor and me speechless until he burst out laughing.

"She doesn't change, does she?"

"No, in fact, I think she might be getting worse."

"Come on then, we'd better not keep her waiting. Have you got everything you need?"

"Yep. Thank you again for this, Connor."

"You can thank me by dancing with me tonight."

"Oh, I don't dance."

"That's okay, neither do I, but I think we can manage a slow dance between us."

"That would be nice."

Connor escorted me out my front door as usual with his hand on my lower back. Today, it helped to calm me and reassure me everything was going to be alright. I really missed it when we reached his car and we had to get in the car. I didn't realise I was so nervous being out all day and night.

When we got to the Fish by the River restaurant and entered the function room where the wedding was to take place, I was blown away by the number of people that were there already. Lacy had really changed the normally plain walls with pictures of local scenes on the wall into a wedding venue. There were fresh flowers on stands around the room and trailing ivy hung from the ceiling down the wall. Chairs were laid out in rows of six on either side, and separated in the middle of the floor was a lovely blue coloured carpet.

"Wow," I couldn't help saying. I was in awe of it all.

"I know, it looks like a florist has had a nervous breakdown in here," Debbie, my non-romantic sister, said.

"Shut up, someone might hear you. I think it looks wonderful!"

Many of the people were wishing David good luck. I hadn't been to many weddings before, but I didn't remember the groom ever looking so nervous. He was shaking, his eyes darting about.

Connor said, "You lovely ladies find a lovely spot for us to sit while I have a chat with the crumbling bridegroom." With that, he went off to join the group of men surrounding David.

He wasn't gone long before the music started, and he sneaked into the place next to me.

Putting his arm on the back of my chair, he whispered to me, "I think David wants everything to be perfect for Jane."

"Does he not realise that as long as he is there, it will be perfect for her?" I whispered back, by which time Jane had entered the room, and holding her uncle's arm, she looked stunning and the picture of happiness. Her dress was ivory with a fitted corset type top with lace over the top which stopped at a ribbon and diamanté belt at the waist. The skirt was lovely and flowing. She didn't wear a veil; instead, her hair was adorned with a tiara.

The wedding was wonderful, and I don't think there were many dry eyes in the place as they said their vows. As they walked back down the aisle together, the love radiating off them both was amazing to see. I was so glad that Jane finally had someone who loved her for the person she was.

A few people had followed behind the wedding party, and as I got up to start the move into the restaurant where the meal was to be had, my body decided at that moment to reject that idea, and I fell back into my seat.

Concern on his face, Connor turned back to me. "Are you okay?" he asked.

"I'm fine. I think my body decided that it liked the chair so much it didn't want to leave it." I tried to give a light-hearted laugh.

Staring down at me with an unamused face, Debbie said, "Don't do that. Don't make a joke of things to hide the truth. You do it all the time, and I bet you don't even notice. Do you need us to help you get up?" Connor looked a bit confused while Debbie said her piece.

"I'm sorry, Debs. Yes. Yes, please, just a little hand." With Connor on my left side and Debbie on my right, they helped me get off the chair.

"Thank you both. I think I got a little numb sitting on the chair and my legs went to sleep."

"Are you sure you're okay?" Connor asked again.

"Yes, thank you, Connor, I am good," I said calmly. "Everything has returned to normal. You can let go if you want."

"Actually, I don't think I do, so I will just keep holding you, if that's alright."

"Emm, okay." I wasn't sure what else to say, nervous about what people would think as we walked into the restaurant hand-in-hand.

The meal was delicious. A seafood platter comprised of prawn cocktail, smoked trout, and mackerel paté with rolls with butter had been placed in the middle of each table for everyone to share, but because Debbie was allergic to prawns, she was given a mini charcuterie board with Parma ham, salami, and a small piece of paté. There were six of us on the table: Connor, Debbie, Rebecca (David's Restaurant manager), Stephen (Jane's ex-fiancé's brother), Chrissy (friend to Jane and waitress at the restaurant), and me. It made the meal and general discussions easy because, other than Rebecca, we had all gone to school with each other.

When she wasn't jumping out of her seat to check on things, Rebecca was joining in as if she had always been part of the group. Connor and I of course knew Rebecca from choir. With the meal finished, it was onto the speeches, starting with Mike, Jane's uncle.

"I remember the day I first met Jane in the hospital the day she was born. When her mum phoned May to tell her to get to the hospital, we were so excited. Packing up James and all his comfort blankets, as he was only six months old, we rushed to the hospital. I was left in the waiting room while your mum and May performed a miracle. I say miracle because that is what you are. I know you are only my niece, but to me, you are my daughter, and I know to James you are the sister he never had. I was so proud to walk you down the aisle, and

I have been so proud in everything you have ever done, as has your aunt." Mike's voice started to shake with emotion as he said this. May held his hand and he smiled down to her. "I do have one warning for you, David, although you might already know this by now, but my niece is the most stubborn person I have ever known, so beware." To which everyone in the room laughed, and there were even a few "hear, hears" shouted from many voices around the room. As we raised our glasses in toast, I took a small sip, because I knew if I had too much to drink, I would really feel it tomorrow, as my body would undoubtedly be sore from pain anyway due to the full day today and I had noticed that my tolerance to alcohol had lessened since my diagnosis.

Next it was David's turn, and he kept his speech short and sweet. "Thank you Mike for your lovely words and I have met Jane's stubborn side and as you know it is as beautiful as she is. I would like to thank you and May for everything you have done for me and Jane and for welcoming me into the family. I know I speak for my wife when I say that we both feel that you are our parents. I would like to thank my best man James, although how much will depend on his speech later. A special thank you from my wife and I goes to Lacy, who has transformed my restaurant into a wonderful wedding venue that neither of us could ever have imagined, and to Rebecca, who is probably not where she should be as she is more of a workaholic than me." He looked over to our table to look for her, but she was on another table checking everything was okay, which yet again filled the room with laughter. She was known for never being able to stay still. "See, what did I say? Anyway, thank you, Rebecca, for making sure everything in the restaurant ran smoothly, and finally, I would like to thank my wife. Thank you for agreeing to marry me. I love you. I would like you to raise your glasses to Jane."

Which everyone did.

Next up was James' speech, who was Jane's cousin and David's best man. He was entertaining as ever, although I think Jane had warned him not to be rude or embarrass her and David, so I think he tried to keep it light as he told a story of their university days. Yet again, he had the room in hysterics. After his story, which was very long, he said, "Now that I have made you all laugh, I want to honestly say: Welcome to the family, David. I have always thought of you as my brother, and I am very happy that it was you who married Jane. I couldn't think of anyone better. Please raise your glasses to the happy couple." Raising our glasses for the final time to the happy couple, the room then burst into a round of clapping, and James decided it was for him and took a bow, which set off out a round of good-natured groans. The room was full of so much happiness you couldn't help but be swept up with it.

Next up was the music, and it started with the bride and groom's dance to A Thousand Years by Christina Perri. Towards the middle of the song, the wedding party joined in: Mike and May, James and Lacy, Rebecca and Keith (the pub manager). The next few songs were upbeat dance songs, and Connor and Stephen got up from the table to go and join the rest of the men by the bar, while Rebecca and Chrissy went to talk with May, which just left me and Debbie at our table.

"Are you okay? I know you're not drinking. Are you not up to it?"

"I'm fine, although I think I might need to move shortly, because otherwise I will get stiff again."

"Okay, why don't we visit the toilets? I could go, and everyone knows girls never go on their own, so it would be the perfect cover."

"That's a good idea. I could do with going as well, only I'm reluctant to get up from this chair in case I fall back into it again."

"It's okay, no one is looking. If you take it nice and slow, you shouldn't have any problems, and I will put my arm in your arm as we walk to the toilet so that you can ease up in your own time."

"Okay, here goes on two - one, two." And with that, I

managed to stand up without falling back, although I was a bit stiff. With Debbie's help, it was a lot easier than I had thought it would be. After the trip to the toilet, we went for a little fresh air outside on the riverbank just to stretch our legs a bit before going back to our table. The others weren't back yet, and just as Debbie poured some more drinks into our glasses, Jane came and sat down in Connor's seat.

"Oh Jane, it was a wonderful wedding, and I love your dress!" I told her.

Taking my hand she said, "Thank you. You and Connor seem to be getting on."

"It's not like that," I replied, but both Jane and my sister looked at each other.

Debbie took me other hand and said, "It may not have started off like that, but I can tell you like him. He is being the perfect gentleman. He keeps giving you covert gazes when he thinks you're not looking and smiles when you are looking."

"I know I have been trying to ignore it, but seriously, what do I have to offer him?"

"Look at me, sister dear, I cannot believe you just said that. You are the better twin, the one who isn't in everyone's face, isn't loud and brash. You have a lot to give someone, if only you could see past your illness and how useless you think it makes you, because you are not useless."

When she had finished her speech, not one of us three didn't have a tear in our eyes.

"We are both perfect in our own way," I replied with a shaky voice.

Then Jane asked the question I was hoping no one would ask. "Have you told him you like him?"

Connor

Walking over to the bar with Stephen to catch up with James and David was my idea, but I didn't want to be too long as Dawn was looking a bit tired. I knew if I asked her if she was alright, she would just force a smile and say everything was fine. I caught up with the guys for a few minutes before my attention turned back towards Dawn. She and her sister were in the midst of a conversation, and all the others had left the table at some point.

James nudged me. "Okay, what's going on with you and Dawn?"

"Nothing."

"Come on, man. I have known you for more years than I

would care to remember, and I have never seen you behave like this towards anyone."

"I like her, okay? But there is something going on with her, and I'm not sure what it is."

"Have you tried asking her?" David asked.

"Of course I have, but each time she just says she's fine."

Both James and David drew a breath, and James said, "You're stuffed, man. I hate it when they use the 'I'm fine' line. It means they are so far away from being fine, but they don't want you to know about it or they think you don't care."

Stephen even joined in, saying, "I don't have a girlfriend, and even I know that when a woman say they're fine it means the total opposite."

"Great, thanks for your help." I turned round to see Dawn gingerly get up from her seat and, arm-in-arm with Debbie, walk towards the toilets. I could see her gait was stiffer than it normally was, but there didn't seem to be any other problems.

I turned back to the others to find them all laughing at me, and as soon as they had stopped being hyenas, the ribbing started. Eventually, when they realised that I wasn't going to rise to their bait, the subject changed to the local football team and their recent win. I just glanced back in time to see Jane walk over to Dawn and Debbie, who had since returned to the table, and sit down with them. I noticed that the only drink Dawn had was water. I decided to check to make sure she didn't want anything else to drink.

I excused myself, and as I got to the table, I heard Jane ask Dawn if she 'had told him yet.' I didn't know what to do, so I just stood where I was in the hopes that I didn't interrupt anything as I eavesdropped on the conversation.

"I can't tell him. I know I need to, but what happens if he looks at me with pity? I couldn't cope with that. I hate that look of pity."

Jane replied, "Connor isn't like that. I think you're just frightened because you don't think you're good enough, but you are! Please give him a chance."

Just as Jane finished talking, she looked over her shoulder and winked at me. I clearly wasn't as invisible as I'd thought, and there was nothing more to do but to continue to the table.

"Ladies," I said as I walked over to Dawn and put my hand on her shoulder. It was only because my hand was on her shoulder that I could feel how tense she was. "Can I get anyone a drink?"

Jane got up and said, "I'm fine, thank you, Connor. I'd better go and mingle."

Debbie also excused herself with the excuse of wanting to talk to someone, which just left me and Dawn at the table.

"Did you want something to drink other than water?"

"Oh no, I'm fine with water. Are you having fun?"

"Yeah! I was just talking to David – apparently pretty soon they will cut the cake, and then they are going to put some slow music on so that I can have that dance you owe me, if you are still up to it?"

"Of course, I would like that," she said with a shy smile. No sooner had she agreed to us dancing than James tapped a knife against a glass to grab everyone's attention. It did not go well as he tapped it a bit too hard and the glass broke - but it certainly got everyone's attention!

Mike shouted, "Now that my son has everybody's attention, it's cake cutting time! So if the bride and groom would come to the cake table while the best man tidies up his mess, we can get this show on the road."

"So romantic," May called across the room to a chorus of laughter.

"You should know I reserve all my romance for you, my love," he called back.

"Mum, Dad, can we not?" James said while rolling his eyes.

"Charmer!" called a voice from the crowd, followed by another bout of laughter.

While everyone was laughing at their antics, David and Jane made their way to the cake table and cut the cake to a round of applause. The cake was then delivered to the tables, and the rest of our table joined us for a slice of the nicest cake I'd had in a long time. The music started up, and again, Stephen asked Chrissy if she would like to dance. Rebecca disappeared, and one of David's friends asked Debbie if she would like to dance, which left me and Dawn alone.

"Shall we take the next dance?" I asked her.

"Umm, okay, as long as it's a slow one."

I stood up to get ready for the start of the next song, but Dawn got up very slowly, as if she needed to tell her body to move. I just waited for her to stand up right before I took her hand to support her and asked her if she was ready.

Just as we got to the dancefloor, the music changed, and David Essex's 'Hold Me Close' came on, so I took Dawn's hand, and together we continued to the dancefloor, where I pulled her towards me so that we were face to face. With one arm around her waist and my other holding her hand, we moved slowly round the dancefloor until we found a quiet space, and we just stayed in that area swaying till the music ended. At the end of the song, we returned to our table to find Debbie sitting and smiling at us.

"You two looked like you were having fun."

Dawn blushed and tried to 'sssh' her sister, but it didn't help, as Debbie said, "I'm going to leave you together for a little longer uninterrupted as there's someone I wanted to talk to." With that, she got up and walked away.

"Subtle, isn't she?" I said to Dawn.

"It's definitely not her middle name. I think David and Jane are leaving shortly, as he's trying to persuade her to stop talking to May," she said as we looked over to watch.

"David said they're off to Paris on their honeymoon. Have you ever been?"

"No, I haven't had the chance to go abroad. I did get a passport in the hopes that it would get some usage, but it hasn't. What about you?"

"I've been too busy working and concentrating on my promotion exams to go anywhere. I was also worried about leaving my mum in case she needed me."

"You are a good son." She smiled at me.

"So she tells me, but most of the men I know would look

after their mum if they were on their own and needed a little help."

"You're probably right, especially around here, but you do realise that if she needed any help, there is a whole village willing to help her."

"She doesn't like asking for help, because she doesn't want to be a burden."

I was sure I heard her mumble, "I know the feeling," but it was so quiet that if I hadn't been looking at her, I wouldn't have caught it. James came round to all the tables to say that the bride and groom were getting ready to leave and that people were going outside to say goodbye. Getting up gingerly on Dawn's behalf, we went to go outside.

When I held her hand again, she said, "Why do you keep holding my hand? People will get the wrong end of the stick. The marriage and pregnancy rumours have just died down; we don't want them to think we are dating again."

"Would that be too far from the truth? I think what we have been doing is a gentler form of dating, just getting to know each other … but I would like to date you properly."

She looked shocked at what I had said. For a second, she looked down at the ground as if she was embarrassed, but then all of a sudden, it was as if she had gathered some inner strength as she lifted her head and looked at me and said, "We need to talk about that."

"I know, and we will, but not tonight. It's getting late and we are both exhausted. Come on, let's say goodbye to the happy couple, and then we can see if Debbie is ready to call it a night."

"Alright."

Half an hour later, I had dropped Debbie off at her house, who left with the words, "Night, lovebirds!" Pulling up to Dawn's drive, I told her to stay there while I jumped out of the car to help her get out. Having watched her all evening, I knew she was starting to slow down. When we got to her front door, she asked me if I wanted to come in.

"No; much that I want to, you have had a busy day and night, so I won't keep you."

She smiled at me gratefully. "I do need to talk to you, though … would you like to pop round tomorrow?"

"That would be lovely. I tell you what, I'm taking Mum and Alan to the pub tomorrow for lunch. We've booked a table, so it won't matter too much if I increase the table size. Why don't you and Debbie join us? And then we can talk afterwards."

"Are you sure your mum and Alan won't mind?"

"They wouldn't have a problem at all. Let me know if Debbie is joining us and then I'll phone the pub to change the booking. It's booked for 12.30; if you need a lift, just let me know."

"Thank you. I'll text her when I get in and let you know. Thank you for everything today. I've had a wonderful time."

"So have I. I will look forward to your message." And with that, I gave her a quick kiss on the lips before I smiled and walked away.

I had just got home when I received the text from Dawn to say that she and Debbie would love to join us for lunch and that Debbie would drive so she didn't need a lift. I quickly phoned the pub before they closed and changed our booking to five people.

The next morning, since Alan was bringing Mum and Debbie was bringing Dawn, I decided I would walk to the pub, as the sun was shining and it was a nice day. I realised it would be my only exercise of the day, so I decided, come tomorrow, I would need to start combined training again, starting with an early morning run, then swim and bike ride. I'd always liked to be competition-ready, even though I didn't do that many triathlon competitions anymore. Exercise would also help clear my head and destress me. Being in the police force wasn't always easy and training helped me focus on other things.

The village was unusually quiet after Jane's wedding, but a few people were out walking. The only topic of conversation was how wonderful Jane's wedding had been.

I got to the pub just before 12.30, just as Debbie pulled up in the car park, so I waited before entering the pub. Alan's car wasn't in the car park, so I knew he hadn't arrived yet. Walking over to Debbie's car, I opened the passenger side door and Dawn looked up and smiled at me.

"Hello Connor," she said, but the smile on her face said so much more as her light blue eyes shone brightly. She certainly looked much better than yesterday when I'd dropped her off.

Helping her out of the car, I kissed her quickly on the cheek and said, "Morning, beautiful."

"What am I, the ugly sister?" I heard her sister say.

"Of course not. Morning, Debbie."

As I looked back to Dawn, we both rolled our eyes at her sister's melodramatics. Just as I closed the passenger door, Alan drove up and parked his car in the free blue badge space.

Getting out of his car, he called, "Morning, everyone! Sorry if we're late."

"You're not. We all just got here."

Walking round to the passenger's side to help my mum get out of the car, he said, "Good, good; your mum was worried we would be late."

As my mum got out of the car, I could see that yesterday had probably been a bit too much for her, which was one of the reasons I'd suggested we had our normal Sunday lunch out today.

Kissing her on her cheek, I asked, "Are you okay, Mum?"

"I'm okay, honey; don't fuss. Alan has been looking after me, and it's nice to be out of the house for a change, although I think yesterday might have been a bit too much, but it was a lovely day, so worth it."

Walking into the pub and saying hello to all the people we knew took a little while, especially as Mum hadn't seen many people for a while and neither had Dawn. I pulled out Dawn's chair just as Alan pulled out Mum's, and it was only at that point when both women sat down that I realised they were mirroring each other in the way that they moved. This led me to think back to Dawn's typical body language, and the more I thought about it, the more I was convinced that Dawn had exactly what my mum had. But I didn't want to bring it up in case I was wrong. It was up to her to tell me when she felt comfortable enough.

Chapter 4

Dawn

The car journey to the pub was a nightmare, as all I kept hearing from Debbie was what a lovely guy Connor was and "You need to tell him about your condition." Eventually, I gave in and told her that it was my intention to tell him later on that day. I didn't want to go further into the relationship without him knowing the truth, and then if he couldn't handle it, we could hopefully just stay friends. It would hurt, but friends would be better than nothing.

As we pulled up to the car park, Connor was waiting for us in a pale blue short-sleeved shirt and blue denim jeans. He looked relaxed as he walked over to where I was sitting in the car and opened the door like the gentleman he was. He leaned over and kissed my cheek. I wished that it had been on my lips, but I knew that we hadn't had a truthful discussion about our relationship yet, although I could feel that we were both on the same page in what we wanted. I just hoped I wasn't wrong. As he greeted us, I looked up and smiled at him and I could feel the tension of the car journey leave me. His smile had that effect on me. As we walked towards the door of the pub, his mum and Alan drove up and parked, and Alan got out of the car and went round to his mum's side, much the same way Connor had done for me.

Walking into the pub, I was surprised by how many people where there, and then it dawned on me that I hadn't had a Sunday pub lunch for ages. After saying hello to some of the people, most of whom we'd seen yesterday at the wedding, we got to the table, where Connor pulled out my chair while I sat down.

He then went round to Debbie's seat, but she told him, "I got it, don't worry about me." I was sat between Connor and Debbie at the round table, then it was Charlotte (Connor's mum) and Alan. I liked being out with Charlotte and Alan. I had known them both for such a long time, as, like many people in the village, we had grown up around them and seen them at May's barbeques, although other than last night and the barbeque the other weekend, I hadn't spent much time talking to either of them. We all decided what we were going to eat. With that decision made, Connor and Alan went up to the bar to order our food and drinks.

"Dawn," Charlotte said. "Can I ask you a personal question?"

I narrowed my eyes with confusion. "Depends on the question."

"How long have you had fibromyalgia?"

I could feel my body start to shake. As I looked down as

my hands and as I thought they were shaking, I didn't know what to say. I was shocked that she had realised that there was something wrong, let alone the fact that she had heard of fibromyalgia. I turned to look at Debbie, who looked as taken aback as me.

"How did you know? I was diagnosed last year."

"I recognised the signs. I've been living with it for more than twenty years. They didn't diagnose me for a long time. I had to go through various tests and saw consultants who were very dismissive of me. It was only because Dr Davies was so determined to help me that I was diagnosed. Is that how it was for you?"

"It took about two years for me to get diagnosed!" I sighed with relief. It was so good to be able to talk openly with someone about my condition. "Dr Davies told me he thought it was fibromyalgia, but that I would have to wait to hear from the rheumatologist. In the end, I just had a telephone call with them, and after a few questions, they confirmed Dr Davies' diagnosis. I initially had counselling and pain clinic appointments, but that has all finished now."

"Yeah, you're just suddenly left to manage it yourself. On the bad days, you need to rely on the people who love you to help, and be around on the good days to make sure you don't overdo it. Does Connor know?"

"Not yet. I was going to tell him tonight."

"I can tell you are nervous, but one thing you didn't know before and you do now is that my boy knows a lot about this condition and has helped me so much through the years. He has done so much research into fibromyalgia he could probably get a doctorate in it! Trust him to do the same for you, and if you ever need to talk to someone who understands and someone who is going through similar things, I am just at the end of a telephone, or you can pop round if you want to. Now, let's change the subject, because they are on their way back."

"Thank you, Charlotte. I appreciate it."

Approaching our table with what could only be described as a cheeky smile on his face, Alan asked, "Is it safe to come back now? Have you ladies finished discussing yesterday's wedding?"

"Oh hush, Alan, we weren't talking about the wedding. That's not all women talk about, now behave," Charlotte replied, rolling her eyes. She gave him a friendly punch on his arm.

I loved the interaction between Charlotte and Alan; they seemed so close, and had obviously known each other for a very long time. I could tell there was also a special bond between him and Connor.

It didn't take long for the food to arrive, and when

we weren't eating, we had a relaxing chat about the latest gossip going around the village and the events taking place at the community centre. It was just what I needed after the excitement from yesterday and dancing with Connor. We left the pub at two o'clock, and I arranged for Connor to pop around at six.

That morning, he had persuaded his friend, a fisherman, to give him some fresh fish. He gave some to his mum and Alan and agreed to cook the rest at mine later, along with some bread.

Debbie drove me home and stayed long enough to have a cup of tea and give me another sisterly lecture about telling Connor about my fibromyalgia, which I reassured her yet again I would. She couldn't understand why I didn't want to shout about my diagnosis from the rooftops, even if it would make things a little bit easier, but it was still hard for me to get my head around my health and all the quirks that each day seemed to bring. The counselling had helped a little, but I still had problems accepting that there were things I couldn't do that people of my age took for granted. Despite knowing that I had her support, I worried that not everyone would be as supportive. I guess hanging around with Sarah (the Greengrove bully who had moved away last year) had rubbed off on me. I was worried that there would be more people who'd think the way she did and that they would look at me differently.

After Debbie left, I managed to have a little nap on the sofa, waking up just in time to have a quick freshen-up before Connor arrived. I didn't know quite how I was going to broach the subject, but after the quick talk with his mum at lunchtime and finding out that she also had fibromyalgia, it really helped put things into perspective because at least I knew that he understood the condition. The big question remained as to whether or not he wanted to be in a relationship with someone with the same condition as his mum or whether he would find it all too much.

Luckily, Connor arrived before I could work myself into a state. Opening the door to see him standing there smiling, holding up a bag of freshly caught fish in one hand and two baguettes in the other with a cheeky grin as he said "Fish delivery!" made me laugh and certainly bought a smile to my face.

"Come in."

As he came in the door, he leaned over and kissed me on the lips, though it was a bit hampered by the baguettes and fish he was holding.

"Hang on, I need to put these down in the kitchen and do that properly," he said with a chuckle.

We walked into the kitchen and he put the food on the

work bench. I asked him, "Do you want a cup of tea?" as I put the kettle on.

I reached over to the peppermint tea bag cannister as he put his arms around my waist. With his chest to my back, he kissed my neck and said, "Yes, please. Peppermint would be lovely. Do you need a hand?"

Smiling over my shoulder to him, I replied, "No, I'm okay, thank you. Why don't you take a seat and I'll be in shortly?" I knew I needed a little breather. I was nervous for this talk to happen. It didn't take long for the kettle to boil and for the tea to be made the way we both liked it. I had made enough for us on a Thursday night after choir to know how Connor preferred it, which was exactly how I preferred mine - not too strong. I took a deep breath and gave myself an internal pep talk that everything would be okay. By the time I got to the living room, Connor could tell that I was nervous, as my hands were shaking carrying the cups of tea. I was glad that I hadn't filled them up too much.

"Are you alright, Dawn?"

Placing the cups down on the coasters and turning to sit next to him on the sofa, I said, "Yes, but there is something I wanted to talk to you about, and I'm a little bit nervous about it because I have never told anyone this before."

Connor took my hands in his and rested them on his lap, twisting himself so that his knees were touching mine. This meant that I wasn't able to keep twisting my fingers, and it stopped them from shaking as well.

"You can tell me anything. I know we are only at the start of our relationship, but we have known each other since we were in nursery school, so take a deep breath and let it out, because I doubt it's going to make me run for the hills … unless, of course, you're a mass murderer and I'm your next victim … then, bye."

Laughing, I said, "Oh, I'd better keep that quiet then! But no, that's not it. I think I've just built this up in my mind to be bigger than it is." I took a deep breath. "I'm not sure where to start … About three years ago, I started to feel unwell. It started off small—it was as if I had a virus I couldn't really get over. I just kept getting tired doing the simplest of things, and I started getting pain in various parts of my body—my knees, my back, and my hands—it was as if my body was getting stiff for no reason. I think I was driving Dr Davies round the bend, as I kept going back to him as I couldn't understand what was going on with me. I had various blood tests, and we tried various pain killers as we tried to get to the bottom of what was going on.

"In the end, I was diagnosed with fibromyalgia." I took a

deep, steadying breath. Saying it out loud was a strange mix of terror and relief. "Not many people know I have it, just Mum and Dad, Debbie, Jane, and now you, and your mum guessed at lunch time."

"Thanks for telling me. But why were you so worried? Did you think it would make a difference to what I feel about you? Because it really doesn't."

"I didn't realise that you knew about fibro till lunch time today when I spoke to your mum." I paused and looked at my feet. "Sometimes it's hard for me to handle my condition, so I thought that if we were to continue going into this relationship, it was best that you knew everything."

"I'm not surprised that mum managed to guess. If I'm honest, I had an inkling that there was something similar about the way you and my mum moved and did things, but I didn't know quite how to broach the subject, so I'm glad that you told me. But it doesn't put me off you, if that's what you're worried about. Yes, I have lived with mum and her fibro for many years, but I have done a lot of research and have been to a lot of her appointments. Of course, that doesn't make me an expert, but it also doesn't put me off being with you … and it certainly doesn't make me feel sorry for you, before you think that as well."

"How did you know that was where my mind was going?"

"Because I know you, and to be honest, that's the sort of thing my mum would think, so I thought I would say it just in case you think alike."

"Oh, I thought maybe it was your great detective skills …"

"Sadly, no, it wasn't! But getting back to the main issue, I am not at all frightened by your condition. It is not you. It is a part of you but it doesn't define you. It isn't the part of you that is funny, kind, intelligent … and various other things that I would mention, but I don't want your ego to get too big." He grinned at me.

"I don't think my ego would get too big, but thank you."

"Can I ask you something?"

"Of course."

"Why do you cover up your condition? Why do only a few people know about it?"

"I don't want people to look at me differently. I had a lot of counselling after I was first diagnosed to help me accept the condition and the limits it sets on my life, listening to my body and such. But I still find it hard saying to people that 'I would love to go out with you tomorrow night but I don't think I can stay past midnight because tomorrow I wouldn't be able to function.'" I sighed. "Luckily, I have Debbie, so she helps me, and we have a system. Because we share the same friends, we tend to get invited to the same things.'

He put his hand over mine and said, "I didn't mean to upset you."

It was at that moment that I realised that tears were on my cheeks and that Connor had released one of my hands to wipe the tears away.

"I have no idea why I'm getting upset about this; it's my life now, and there's not a lot I can do about it."

"I think my mum felt like this when she was diagnosed, and sometimes she still does. I'm not sure one hundred percent because I was only a child. My dad had died, and she was a single parent left with this illness she couldn't control, so things were hard for her, and she got depressed. But from what I understand, that can be quite common because of the complexities of this condition. I think it would be a good idea, if you want, to chat to her. The counselling is all well and good, but it's better talking to someone who has actually gone through the same thing as you."

"She did offer to meet up with me, and it would be nice to talk to someone who has been through some of the same things and has the wisdom to say, 'Been there, done that, got the t-shirt'."

"Please don't tell her she has wisdom! I will never hear the end of it! Now, why don't we have some dinner, then we can discuss our next night out?"

"Okay," I said with a sheepish grin and a sigh of relief.

Just then, my phone on the coffee table flashed up with a text from Debbie.

Have you told him yet????

We both looked over to it, and I don't think I had ever gone so red with embarrassment. Connor just laughed.

"I am going to kill her."

"It's not that bad, honestly. I take it she was making sure you weren't going to wimp out of telling me?"

"She wouldn't listen when I kept telling her I was going to tell you tonight."

"Shall we shut her up for a little while?"

"Oh, I would love that. What are you thinking?"

"We can ring her on your phone, but I will speak to her—she won't be expecting that."

"She really won't. Okay, let's do it."

I put her on speaker phone and the moment she

answered, we both heard her bellow down the line, "Dawn, I swear, if you are ringing to tell me you haven't told him, I don't know what I am going to do!"

"Don't get your knickers in a twist, Debbie, she has told me, and in a minute, we are going to be sitting down to some nice fresh fish and baguettes with wine. Are you going out tonight and enjoying yourself?"

Debbie fell silent then quietly said, "Errrmmm, I was thinking of going to the pub, but I wanted to make sure everything was ok?"

"Everything is fine. You go out and enjoy yourself tonight. Have the night off from worrying about Dawn, and Dawn can have the night off from worrying about you. What do you think?"

"Umm. Okay. As long as you are sure everything is okay. Umm, pass me to my sister?"

"You're on speaker phone, Debbie," I said, suppressing a giggle.

"Ah. Right. Love you, Dawn. Phone me tomorrow?'

"Will do, love you too, have a great night."

We disconnected the phone call and burst out laughing.

"Are you two always like that?" Connor asked.

"Oh, yes. But being twins, I can sometimes work out what she's going to say before she actually says it. Sometimes in my head, I think to myself, please don't say it, please don't, and then she does and there's nothing I can do about it but wait for the repercussions."

"Right, come on, let's get our dinner sorted, and while we are eating you can tell me more about your twin-hood."

It was the nicest fish platter I'd ever had, consisting of prawns, salmon, and crab, and tuna paté with baguette.

I regaled him with 'oh no she didn't' stories concerning my sister, some of which he had heard of before, as we had gone to the same schools. He still remembered when she'd tried to audition to play Sandy in Grease, and he joked that it had taken hm six months before his hearing ever came back properly.

Like every night I had spent with Connor, the hours just flew by, and before we knew it, midnight was upon us. I was conscious of the fact that Connor had work early in the morning, and although we had just been sitting talking, I was getting tired, and I knew that he was aware of this as well.

"Right, I'd better be going. I have an early morning shift tomorrow and you need your sleep."

"I didn't realise tonight had gone so fast!"

"It normally does when I'm with you. Now, I don't want you to do any more worrying about us. I will try to text you during my lunch hour tomorrow, but it will depend on how busy it is. Failing that, I will ring you when I finish work."

"I'll try not to worry. Speak to you tomorrow."

Connor kissed me and wrapped me in his arms, squeezing me tightly enough to make me feel cherished but not enough to hurt me.

It was only after he left that I realised how tired I was. With the wedding and the trip to the pub, a lot of spoons had been used up in a forty-eight hour period. Unfortunately, I had a mini-flare-up for about two weeks. We never really went out on a date, unless you included going to choir, because the pain and tiredness was just too much. I was just having to use all the energy I had on work, but Connor didn't mind. When he could, he came round to my house and either cooked dinner or brought a takeaway. On Thursday nights, he took me to choir and brought me home, staying long enough to make sure I got into bed, and he never complained once.

Chapter 5

Three Months Later

Dawn

I didn't need to worry, as, just like Connor's mother and Debbie had said, he didn't treat me any different knowing the truth, and with his shifts and my work commitments, we had fallen into a pattern. On a Thursday before choir, he would come to my house and we would have something light before we went to sing. He continued to train for his triathlon before and after his shifts and on his days off. I don't know where he found the energy, I could only be proud of the fact that he did.

We had just finished choir practice when I decided that I would ask him if he wanted to stay over tomorrow night. This would be the first time that he would stay, and I was nervous, but I knew that Connor was letting me lead our relationship. He parked his car on my drive.

"Are you coming in?"

"I am, if it's all right with you?"

"Yes, there is something wanted to ask you."

With that, he got out of the car and came round to the

passenger door to help me out of the car. Walking into my house. I asked him if he wanted a drink, to which he declined. Sitting on the sofa, I took a deep breath.

"I wanted to ask you a question."

"Okay."

"Tomorrow night, I wondered if you wanted to stay the night, as I know you are off on Saturday and me and Debbie are off out at the spa using the vouchers that we had bought each other for our birthdays. So it will be a little relaxed morning. I understand it you don't want to, there's no pressure."

"Dawn?"

"Yes?"

"Ssshh I would love to stay over tomorrow night, I think it's a great idea. Why don't you tell me about the trip to the spa?"

"That's great. It's a tradition we started when we turned twenty-one, and it means that for one day a year, we get to be truly pampered and spend quality time together."

"That sounds like a wonderful idea, and I bet it truly relaxes you."

"It does, to be honest. I look forward to it so much. What were your plans for Saturday?"

"I am going to spend the day with my mum after I have done some training, then in the evening, I am going out with James and David and a few of the boys."

"Oh, I wonder if the girls want to come over here for a drink while you are on your boys' night out. I will send them a text."

Not long after that was sorted and the girls had responded that they were up to come to mine, Connor left to go home and I went to bed. It was only then that the nerves started to hit home. Sleep was hard to come by because I was worried about so many things that shouldn't have mattered, such as 'I hope he isn't disappointed that I am not a night owl', 'I hope I don't get stressed too much', 'I hope he finds the bed comfortable' and the stupidest thing of all, 'I hope the water pressure in the shower is okay'. I mean, what was I going to do if it wasn't? Talk about over-thinking things.

Connor

I was happy going at Dawn's pace as far as this relationship was concerned. I preferred it. Although we had known of each other for years, taking it slowly meant that we were spending time becoming real friends and getting to know each other in a more in-depth way than I had ever known any other woman. Mum said she and my Dad had been the same.

I was only too happy to share our relationship details with mum; we had been a team since Dad had died, and Mum really understood Dawn's condition.

Dawn's acceptance of what she could and couldn't do made our relationship a bit of an exploration for both of us. We were fitting into each other's lives like jigsaw pieces, and it felt so right.

The next step came when Dawn asked me to stay over. It would be the first time I would stay over, and the next day I was off work, and I knew that we both had a very busy Saturday. I wanted to make sure that there were no misunderstandings with what she wanted and that we were on the same wavelength when it come to the next steps.

I arrived at her house after work with my overnight bag and carrying the fresh bread we'd always eat before choir. I know I bought some yesterday as it was choir yesterday, and we always tended to opt for something quick, like bread & cheese, paté, or some soup, rather than a big meal. Normally, if we were having bread, I would order it from the shop in the morning; they'd keep it aside for me. I knew that we had eaten yesterday's all up, but I thought that there was no harm in grabbing another one on the way over; one of the joys of village living. But I'd also bought some iced buns that Mum had made, which we could have afterward. Opening the door to me, Dawn stood there dangling a key on her finger. Well, I guess that answered the question as to whether we were on the same wavelength or not.

"What's that?"

"I wanted to give you a key to my house. We have been dating for more than three months now, and it seems silly that every Thursday when I know you are coming round you have to knock on the door to be let in. This way, you can just let yourself in."

I was taken aback. I hadn't expected that. Although it made sense in what she was saying, I'd thought we were a long way from swapping keys. Not that I minded; in fact, I was over the moon and couldn't help the smile that was probably a mile long on my face.

"Thank you. Now come here, I haven't even had a kiss yet or the opportunity to tell you that you look beautiful today."

I put down my bag just inside the front door and took her into my arms, kissing her with a hello. I did just as I promised. After kissing her, I looked at her and I said to her, "You look beautiful today."

"You say that every day, even when you don't see me."

"I know, and it's always true."

Laughing, she said to me, "You charmer." Taking the key and putting it on my key ring while Dawn prepared the food and brought it into the living room, I went back into the kitchen to make sure she didn't need a hand before I carried our hot drinks into the living room. We really were like a well-oiled machine.

Sitting on the sofa, I wanted to broach the subject of me staying the night.

"So tonight… you know it's alright you know if you change your mind at any time, and even if I do stay the night, nothing has to happen. I can sleep on the sofa if you want."

"Well, that sounds very boring, and Debbie will be very disappointed tomorrow when she tries to get the juicy details out of me and I'll have to say 'Well, we watched a film and ate some dinner, we kissed, and then he slept on the sofa.' I'm not going to change my mind," she said stubbornly. "I want this more than anything, Connor. Please don't make me tell my sister you slept on the sofa." She fluttered her eyelids at me. In all honesty, all it did was make us both laugh.

"Thank heavens you said that. I was just being chivalrous. I mean, your sofa is comfortable enough to sit on, but I'm not sure I could fit sleeping on it."

"That's one of the things I love about you, you're self-sacrificing."

She looked shocked as she realised what she had said. She was just about to backtrack when I said to her, "Nope, don't you dare. I am not having you changing your mind or rethinking what you just said. Are you worried that it's too early to say that there are things about me that you love? Because it isn't. There are things about you that I love, and if I am being completely honest I am falling in love with all of you, even though it hasn't been long since we started going out with each other. I don't think we should measure things by time. I think it should be measured by how we are feeling."

"I think you are right."

"Good, now come here and tell me some more things that you love about me."

"Nope, you will have to wait until I drop a few more things into conversations."

"Spoilsport."

"I don't want your head to get too big."

"Fair enough."

Having finished dinner and tidied up, we decided what film we were going to watch. In the end we decided on a detective film. As usual with Dawn, the night was filled with fun and laughter. We had watched a few films together before, and each time we watched them we became more of a film critic, especially if it was something we knew about.

As time went on and the film was nearing its end, I expected her to be nervous about me staying the night, because I knew I was, but if she was, she didn't show it. In fact, by the time the film ended, all she said was that she was tired. She said, "I know it's only nine o'clock and probably too early for you, but is it alright if I go to bed?"

"I am tired as well, so I think that's a great idea. Is it alright if I come to bed too?"

"Of course, come on, let's go to bed."

"Okay, I will lock up and be with you in a minute. Do you want some water or anything?"

"Oh, yes, please."

"No problem."

She disappeared upstairs to the bedroom, and I checked all the windows and doors were closed before getting our water. By the time I got to the bedroom, she had already got changed into her nightclothes and was just entering the ensuite to brush her teeth. While she was in there, I got into my sleep shorts, and when she came out of the bathroom, I changed places with her. Meanwhile, she jumped into bed.

Leaving the en suite, I found her on the left side of the bed, sitting up.

"I hope it's okay if I sleep on this side, but I can sleep on the other side if you prefer."

"No, the right side is perfect."

Getting into bed, I pulled her close to me. "Are you okay?" I asked her.

"I'm great, and strangely, I'm no longer tired."

"Are you not? I wonder what I can do to tire you out?" I winked at her.

"I wonder," she replied with a smile and a glint in her eyes. I bent my head down and started off kissing her gently, but very quickly the kisses turned more ferocious, which she returned. My hands were all over her body, taking off her bedclothes. We were both on edge. There was no way I could step away from her, not tonight.

I kissed her. Scratch that. I devoured her, owning that kiss, capturing every ounce of passion. I'd wanted to kiss and touch and explore her for weeks, and now I wasn't going to hold back any longer. I was going to make Dawn mine.

As I traced around her breast with my forefinger, then mapped the same spot with my mouth, she shuddered, and I knew she was going to give in to whatever I asked of her tonight.

"You're beautiful, Dawn," I whispered, cupping her breast, flicking her nipple with my finger while making eye contact so my intentions were clear. Every inch of her was mine to pleasure tonight. Her breathing accelerated.

Bending at the waist, I kissed between her breasts, moving slowly under the right one, licking the underside and then kissing it back up on the side. I felt her contract the muscles of her stomach as if she was bracing herself and expected me to do more. I was going to move further down, but I wasn't done with her breasts yet. They were so perfect and delicious.

"I'm going to explore every inch of you."

"Every inch?" she whispered in return. "That might take a long time."

"I'm not in a hurry, are you?"

"Connor," her voice shook when I moved to her left breast, giving it the same attention with my hands, but instead of flicking her nipple with my thumb, I captured it in my mouth. She gasped, rocking up and down on her toes.

I looked up at her while I moved my mouth down to her stomach, slowly circling her stomach and beyond, her belly pebbled with goosebumps. She wanted me just as much as I wanted her; I could tell by the way her body reacted to me with each kiss I placed on her, and each time her body involuntarily came towards me, begging me for more, and each little noise I could hear her make. Her responses were driving me mad. I couldn't wait any longer. "Are you sure this is still okay?"

"Yes Connor, please."

I needed to be inside her.

I watched her face as I entered her. I wanted to see all her reactions, to commit them to memory, to know everything she liked and do it again and again and again. I only moved slowly until I was fully inside her. Again I asked if she was okay, although I was unsure as to what I would do if she said no; but, luckily, with a smile and a nod, my control was lost. I moved faster and faster; there was nothing I could do. I couldn't slow down; the feeling was just too intense. We were just too perfect together, and I could tell by the expression on her face, which radiated calmness and peace, that she felt the same. It was as if we had found something we didn't know was missing until that very moment. Just when I felt that it couldn't get any better, we both exploded at the same time, and for the first time ever, I nearly blacked out. It was as if fireworks had exploded in my head, and my legs were burning. Every muscle clenched in my body.

When I was able to move, I lay next to her and pulled her close to me and said, "Are you okay?"

"I'm better than okay … but … I can't think at the moment," was her reply.

Waking up in the morning, Dawn's head was still resting on my shoulder and her hand was resting on my stomach. I kissed the top of her head, whispering her name in the hopes that I could wake her up gently. We both had a busy day ahead and I wanted to fix her breakfast before I went out.

Dawn

I was awoken by Connor kissing my head and whispering my name. There are worse ways to wake up.

"Morning," I mumbled as I smiled up to him.

"Morning," he said with a smile. "I thought I would make you some breakfast before you went. Would you like that?"

"Well, that would be nice … but I suppose that means I would have to leave this really comfy place."

"Sadly, it does, yes."

He tickled me so that I would move off him, but before

he left the bed, he leaned over and kissed me. One thing led to another, and eventually we left the bed later than he'd anticipated, but neither of us were complaining.

While I had a shower, Connor made breakfast. Connor had finished his shower and was just dishing up his omelette when Debbie arrived. Letting herself in as usual, she found me and Connor in the kitchen as I was just pouring us a cup of coffee.

"How are the lovebirds this morning?"

"Morning, Debbie," we both answered at the same time which led us both to laugh.

"Ahh, it's so sweet; you are even speaking at the same time."

"Can I cook you an omelette?" Connor asked.

"No thanks, I will just have some toast. I hope you have been looking after my sister."

"Debbie, boundaries!" I shouted at her.

"What? I am only looking out for you," she replied, looking innocent—which is one thing my sister definitely wasn't.

After breakfast, Connor tidied up, then got ready to

leave. After some more ribbing from Debbie, which Connor took all on the chin, we all left around 10.30. Debbie's and my first treatment started at 11.00.

No sooner had I got in her car than Debbie started with the questioning. "So how was it? I know you were nervous."

"You were right," I admitted, rolling my eyes. "I worried over nothing, it was absolutely perfect, and he was a real gentleman. He even offered to sleep on the sofa in case I had changed my mind."

"I need a man like that! Why could his mum not have had two sons?"

"There has to be more men like that out there somewhere. You found him once, you will find him again."

"We're not talking about him. You promised never to mention his name again."

"Technically, I didn't mention his name," I huffed. "There is a man out there for you, I just know it."

"Come on, let's have a day with no male interference. First up, massages, then nails and pedicure."

Entering the spa, it was lovely and relaxing, the smell

of vanilla and sandalwood really helped to soothe your mind and your senses. We were greeted by the receptionist, who took our names and showed us to the changing rooms where we got ready for our massages. Hanging our coats and bags away with our phones, we were each called away by our massage therapists. Mine was called Pam and Debbie's was called Svetlana. We each went into a different room. In my room with Pam, I went over my fibromyalgia and what type of massage I was looking for and what type of pressure I was looking for. All the way through the massage, she kept checking to make sure that everything was alright and that the pressure was alright. I knew that some people with fibromyalgia didn't like massages, but today I could cope with them. I am not sure that if I was flaring I could, but today it was just what I needed. Debbie and I didn't see each other again until we came together for a light lunch, where Debbie started trying to get more information on my relationship with Connor.

"Come on then, tell me how your night with Connor was."

"I'm not telling you that."

"Please! You owe me. If it wasn't for me you wouldn't have got together."

"How do you work that out?"

"I pushed you to go to choir. Not only that, I have to live vicariously through you because I'm not in a relationship."

"I don't think that's how it works."

I didn't plan on telling her everything. She might have been my twin, but I still had my own little secrets. I also wasn't going to give in easily. I knew Debbie; if I told her too much straight away, she would spend the whole time asking questions, so I was best off limiting the amount of time she had to ask the questions by controlling the narrative.

Picking up a sandwich, I said to her, "These sandwiches are lovely. The bread is so fresh. This is much better than the place we went to last year"

"Yes, it is."

"How's work?"

I started by directing her to talk about work, which distracted her through lunch, then we moved to the room where we were having the manicures and pedicures together, but I couldn't hold her off anymore.

"By the way, I knew what you were doing trying to distract me with questions about work, and I let it slide while we ate lunch, but I want all the juicy details now. So come on, let it out and share with your favourite sister."

"You're my only sister."

"As I said, favourite, so come on out with it. Tell me what happened."

"I am not sharing the ins and out of my sex life with you."

"Oh, so there were ins and outs, were there?" she said with a cheeky grin.

"You are unbelievable. You knew that wasn't what I meant."

"I know, sorry not sorry. Were you nervous? After your diagnosis, being physical in a relationship was one of the things you were worried about."

"I wasn't nervous at all. Connor was so good, it was as if he could read my mind. He kept checking in with me, and he was attentive, even this morning. He kept everything relaxed, which was why he made me breakfast, so I didn't need to do anything, just get ready in my own time. There was no pressure. I really think I've just been with the wrong men in the past, because I have never been with anyone who has been so relaxed and attuned to what I need."

"I'm glad. You deserve it."

"Thank you, but so do you. We just need to find your man."

Having finished our pampering, we drove home. Jane and Lacy were coming to my house for dinner and drinks. This would only be the third time we had got together as a foursome, and the first time since Jane had got married. It was hard to believe that, when we had been growing up, we'd allowed one person to have so much say in who we'd interacted with, and because of this we hadn't really spoken to Lacy much. But it also meant that Debbie, Jane, and I had missed out on a really good friend and an amazing woman. But we were righting that wrong now, and we were all very glad that Lacy had forgiven us for the stupid and cruel things we had done when we were younger.

We had just opened the bottles of wine when Jane and Lacy arrived. Having poured everyone a glass, we got down to the serious business of deciding what takeaway we were going to have for dinner. With Chinese chosen, we placed our order and snacked on some nuts while we waited the hour for it to arrive. We had a normal catch-up session, chatting about our work: Jane as a teacher, Lacy as an event planner, Debbie as a nurse, and me as a project manager.

"I was wonder if next time we get together we could invite Rebecca? She is still fairly new to the village, and would love to be invited along with us, if that's alright with everyone," Jane said.

"Having met Rebecca at choir and at the wedding, I think that would be a great idea. The more the merrier, as far as I am concerned," I replied.

"I think that's a great idea. I really like Rebecca, but she's more of a workaholic than David. Will she be able to get time off work?" Lacy asked Jane.

"David and Rebecca have promoted Chrissy, which means she now covers for both of them occasionally as they both realised that the amount of work they did was unsustainable."

Everyone agreed that was a good idea, and Jane was going to invite Rebecca, as she was the closest to her.

As soon as the Chinese arrived, we set it out on the coffee table so that everyone could pick and choose what they wanted. Like my sister, the girls wanted the details on my relationship with Connor.

"So come on, then. Tell us what is going on with you and Connor," Lacy said.

I couldn't help smiling.

"He's perfect. When I told him about my diagnosis, he just accepted it. He's so good to me when I don't feel so good. He does the little things for me, and he's he so considerate—always asking me if I am okay, which you would think would drive you round the bend, but it doesn't. I really like it because it shows me he cares."

Both Jane and Lacy were throwing in comments about the nice things that James and David did for them.

In the end, Debbie said, "Please tell me it's not all hearts and flowers and that they do some things wrong?"

Lacy replied, "Oh yes, I remember when I heard James tell Peter that he wasn't serious about me and he was only having a laugh with me, biding his time for someone else. I was so in love with him, and I overheard this. I was heartbroken. In the end, I left him a note and went and stayed in a hotel. I had to get away. He kept ringing me, but I didn't answer. I had no one to talk to and I was heartbroken. He found me and explained that he didn't want to tell Peter he loved me before he'd told me, and after a very long talk and a lot of grovelling on his part, I forgave him."

"I didn't know any of that," Jane said. "I would have been there for you if I'd known." She shook her head with disappointment. "Even David messed up once. He kept secrets that he had been receiving calls and text messages from his ex-wife, who had decided she wanted to get back together with him. I only found out about it when his ex-wife turned up on the doorstep. After Peter, I couldn't deal with any more secrets. He had to do a lot of grovelling and promised not to keep anything from me again. At least I had Auntie May to talk to, and James, who had met the ex-wife, who really was a piece of work."

Taking a sip of her wine, Debbie said, "I'm glad these men aren't always perfect! It means there is hope out there for me to find someone. The only problem is, I normally find the most imperfect men with only a hint of perfection, rather than the perfect men with a hint of non-perfection. At least if Connor mucks up, Dawn won't be on her own."

Both Jane and Lacy said at the same time, "No, she won't!"

Lacy added, "You just need to let us know, and the drinks will be brought round and we will be here with a shoulder to cry on, ready to man-bash, as all girlfriends should do."

With that, we all toasted our glasses.

The rest of the night was taken up with Jane talking about her newly married life and the choir. Just as the last of the wine was poured out, the front door was opened. Connor stepped in, and David and James came in to take their wives home.

James asked Debbie if she needed them to walk her home.

She raised her wine glass and replied, "No, that's okay. I'm staying here tonight, so these two need to keep it down tonight."

"Debbie!" I shouted, but everyone else just laughed. I went bright red and hid my face in Connor's chest. Even he was laughing as I could feel his chest rise up and down with laughter. There were times when I could have killed my sister.

Lacy and Jane gave Debbie and me hugs goodbye, and as soon as the front door was closed, I thumped her on the arm.

"I can't believe you said that! You are unbelievable. One day, I'm going to get my own back, big time. And not only that, but it's also nice of you to invite yourself to stay. You can make your own bed up for that. You know where everything is."

"What did I say?"

"I am not falling for that! You know exactly what you said." I narrowed my eyes at her. "Right, off to bed for you before you say anything else."

"Yes, Mum. Night, Connor."

While I was talking to Debbie, Connor was cleaning up, and Debbie went off to the spare room where the sofa bed was. She knew where all the bedding was, so she could sort herself out.

Connor came towards me with our glasses of water.

"Come on, gorgeous, let's go to bed. Don't forget, we need to make a lot of noise just to please Debbie," he said with a chuckle.

"Oh, don't you start."

Waking up with Connor in my bed really was a lovely way to start the day, but he was the only one to get ready for his shift, which started at eight o'clock, whereas Debbie and I were only going shopping at some point. He brought me a mug of coffee in bed and kissed me. Before he left, he promised to text me when he finished work. We hadn't really discussed plans for the week, but I knew he had a few late shifts coming up, so things would have to be a bit more flexible. I didn't mind because it took the pressure off me entertaining. It also meant that he wasn't reliant on me and I wasn't reliant on him. We were, after, all our own separate people.

During the week, as I thought would be the case, I didn't see much of Connor due to his work pattern. We did text and call each other when possible. During one of the phone calls he noticed that I sounded distant.

"Are your pain levels bad?" he asked with a concerned voice.

"I am in a bit of pain and I have had some trouble

sleeping. I think because I am stressed about this project I need to do for work that my body is telling me to calm down and slow down."

"What is it that has you so stressed about it?"

"I think it's because this will be the first time I will lead the report since I took over as project manager. I did some when I was assistant, so I know I can do it, but for some reason I am just panicking about this one."

"I think that's understandable, although, as you have said, you know you can do it. I wish I could come and see you, but I am at work when you are supposed to be sleeping and vice versa. I am not a fan of these shifts, and that's the first time I have ever said that."

"I know."

"Although I am hoping to get away for choir, as I have some time owing, but it will depend on workload. I will let you know, obviously. I miss you."

"I miss you, too."

"I want you to go to bed early. I know you might not fall asleep, but it might help you to relax. Remember, I am so proud of you, and you can do this job. You know you can. I better go."

"Bye."

Unfortunately, he didn't even manage to get away for choir on Thursday night, so Jane came and picked me up and dropped me off so that I didn't miss it as well. When I spoke to him the following Monday, he suggested that we go out for dinner before choir the next Thursday to make up for not seeing him that week. On Wednesday, Connor's mum rang me.

"Hi Dawn, it's Charlotte. I hope it's okay to ring you."

"Of course, it's lovely to hear from you."

"Is now a good time? I am not disturbing you or anything?"

"No, of course not. Are you alright?"

"Oh yes, dear. I just wondered if you wanted to come to the garden centre with me on Saturday."

"Oh, I would love to. I haven't been for ages. Debbie doesn't like going, so I don't like asking her."

"That's great. I don't like going on my own. I will come and pick you up around 11 if that's alright."

"That's perfect; see you then."

"Bye."

I was really looking forward to seeing Charlotte and spending time with her on Saturday.

Chapter 6

Dawn

Going out for dinner was a luxury, especially on a workday, not because of the money but because of the amount of energy it would use up. So when Connor suggested going out to the pub before choir practice on Thursday instead of having a little snack at my house first, I was a little surprised, especially as he was normally so understanding as to how tired I could get, but I didn't want to make a big thing about it, so I agreed.

Due to Connor working the weekend, he was off work that Thursday, so he was going to pick me up at 4.30. I could finish work early because I had some hours owing.

We were to have an early dinner before going on to choir. We decided to go to the Greengrove Arms, and as usual when entering the pub, no matter the time of day, it was like entering a family house, as there were always people ready to welcome you. As we walked in the door, Stephen from the DIY shop was the first to greet us with talk about some village gossip, which was totally made up as usual. It didn't take long listening to Stephen before he saw someone else who hadn't heard his story so we were free to leave and continue towards the bar. Connor turned to me and said, "They say women gossip; they haven't met Stephen."

"I know," I replied. We ordered our drinks and our meals and went to the table that Connor had reserved for us. It was one of the tables by the lovely log fire, which was very welcome, as the day was quite cold. No sooner had we sat down than James came over. "It's okay, I won't stay long. I was on my way home to Lacy and saw you, so thought I would pop and say hello before I left."

"Hello, James. It's good to see you," I said to James just as Connor stood up to shake his hand and say hello to him.

"Right. I have been polite; now it's time to go home to my lovely wife."

"Give Lacy our love."

"I will do, you two have a good night." With that James was gone.

We didn't have a lot of time to talk before choir started, so we rattled through the niceties before getting to the deeper topics.

"Did you have a nice day off?" I asked him.

"I did, but I'm still in training for the North West Triathlon at the end of next month, so I spent a lot of time in the gym and out on the road running."

"So, it was quite a relaxing day off then?" I said with a laugh.

He chuckled. "How was work? Did you manage to finish your report?"

During one of our phone calls last week, I'd told him that I would have to spend most of this week writing my first report on a new project we had just taken on which would be due in today. I had been worried about getting it in on time, as it was an important but complex report and it would be the first time I had to write a report like that. I'd been a bit frightened that I wouldn't be able to deliver what they wanted. I was amazed that he had remembered, especially as he hadn't asked about it all week.

"I did, thank God! My manager phoned, and she was blown away with the amount of work I had put into it. She said it was the most comprehensive report they'd ever had."

"That's great! I know you were worried about it."

"I was. You were right the other day on the phone; I could do it, and I really appreciate you being my sounding board. Thank you."

"No problem, and each one you do it will get easier."

"I know. Anyway, now that's out of the way. I don't know

if your mum told you, but I spoke to her yesterday, and we arranged to go out to the garden centre on Saturday."

"She did tell me. It will do both of you good." He sighed. "She is just coming through a flare-up, and I know I don't need to tell you what that feels like, but even though she has had her fibro for years, it is still hard each time she has an episode. At least now she doesn't overdo it like she used to when I was younger and I didn't understand what was going on. I think some of that was my fault as well because, after my dad died, there was just me and her, and although I knew she wasn't well, I was still a typical teenager in some aspects; things like when I needed my sports kit cleaned for the next day and I couldn't understand why it couldn't be done there and then.

"Once, I remember walking into our house with James and May was round visiting mum, who was crying on the couch. "May turned round and looked at James and I in our football kits, which were covered in mud, and she said to us, 'Don't tell me you both need them clean for tomorrow?'

'Umm, yes,' we'd both replied at the same time.

"May told me to get my spare uniform and go back to James' house because I was having a sleepover and she would wash my kit there. It was only as I got older that I realised the sleepovers and the kit washings happened when my mum had a flare. Her friends would help her during the day and May would help with me in the evening and ensure that I had a normal teenage life."

"We have been talking a lot about the early years of her diagnosis," I said, "and it has been helping me get my head around everything and ask for help. She did mention that she didn't know what she would have done if it wasn't for May and her friends. She also said that I'm not to ignore it if people offer to help. She said I'm not a burden and people wouldn't offer if they didn't want to help, which is something Debbie is always trying to say to me."

At that moment, our meal had arrived. Connor had a Thai beef salad and I had ordered a pumpkin pasta.

"Dawn, I had an idea," Connor said between mouthfuls. "I remember you saying that you liked pop rock music. There is a band playing at the theatre in Helmslade next month. They're really good. They are from round here and you might have heard of them, because they are on the radio sometimes. They are called We Rock. They have a new song out, but they play a mix of old and new songs. It should be a great night out. I thought we could drive and maybe stay near the venue overnight so you don't get too tired. What do you think?"

"I love We Rock, I have all their songs on my playlist but I'm not sure …" I said, staring into my plate of food. I hated disappointing people like this. "I don't tend to get on very well with theatres and concerts. Debbie organised for me to go to a concert for Christmas and she booked us access tickets and they were right at the front, which was really good, and the theatre staff really looked after us, but as soon as the band came on, lots of people came running to the front of the stage and dancing so we couldn't we see … and there was this woman who was jumping up and down like a maniac, and every time she moved backwards, she landed on my foot then fell over backwards and landed on my knee, which, as you can imagine, kicked off the pain big time. In the end, we had to leave.

"We tried again for our birthday and went to the theatre instead, and I would like to say that was better, but honestly it wasn't. We were sat underneath the aircon, so although I had my coat on, I was freezing. Because we were in the middle of the row, the amount of times we had to keep getting up was unbelievable, and, you guessed it, I lost count of the number of people who stood on my toes of dug their elbows into my ribs as they walked past. At the end, you would have thought there was a fire in the building, people couldn't get out of there quickly enough, and I was nearly trampled on. Someone pushed me over as we went up the stairs, so I fell and couldn't get up until Debbie came to the rescue."

"Okay, fair enough. I'm not surprised you are worried about going to the theatre after that. But if I promise nothing like that is going to happen, would you like to go?"

"Other than wrapping me in bubble wrap, I don't know how you can prevent it, although I trust you and would love to go to the theatre with you. I just really don't feel comfortable going to theatres and concerts."

"Please, if I arrange for everything, I guarantee you will have a good night and you won't be harmed all night. If you don't like it, we can leave whenever you like."

I grimaced and gave myself a moment to think. With a sinking feeling, I said with trepidation, "Okay … I will give it a go … I hate that I have had to stop going to places I used to enjoy because of other people's behaviour."

"That's great. You won't regret it. We will have a lovely night, I promise. Now, we'd better hurry up or Jane will have our guts for garters if we are late."

We were the last to arrive at choir, and as usual, it was a great laugh. It seemed Jane really did want the choir to be fun for everyone. At the end of the night, before everyone went home, Jane asked to speak to everyone standing around. Jane stood there with some papers in her hand. "Some of you will remember that when I restarted the choir I said that we wouldn't be entering the traditional choir that the old choir master liked to enter and everyone agreed. I have found a competition that might fit us. It seems to fit within our style of music and I think it will be fun. I have printed off some details for everyone to have a look through. There is no pressure, and if people don't want to do it we don't have to do it. I know I have said this before, but I am going to say it again: I am not in charge of the choir, we all are. So read through everything and let me know what you think."

With that everyone took a sheet of paper and left.

On the drive home, Connor asked me what I thought about the competition.

"I think it would be a really good idea, but personally, I'm scared that I won't be able to do it and I will let everyone down because of a flare-up. You know as well as I do that stress can cause a flare-up... What do you think?"

"I had a quick scan through the information Jane printed off and it all seems quite easy. You film a demo, send it off, then if you qualify, you're given music to learn, then you go to this theatre in Yorkshire, and then there's a live show where everyone sings."

"I thought you only had a quick scan through?"

"I'm so used to gathering information at work quickly that I just grabbed the headlines."

Pulling up to my house, Connor parked in the drive. I'd given up my car two years before when I'd first started feeling unwell. I didn't think I could drive safely, and living in the village, I could get a lot of things locally anyway, so having a car seemed like an unnecessary extra.

Connor was staying tonight, as he normally did when he was on the week five shift. He wasn't needed at work till ten tomorrow, and he'd finish at eight.

Chapter 7

Three months later

Connor

The trip to the theatre had arrived. I knew Dawn was worried about it, but hopefully, I had thought about everything. I had taken mum to the theatre a few times but that was to see a show. But this was different because we were seeing a band, so it was more like a gig, so I could understand why she was worried. But what she didn't know was that I actually knew a few of the band members, so I had some special things arranged for us. Without this bonus, I wasn't sure I would have suggested going.

I arranged to pick her up on Saturday at 4.30, but I gave her strict instructions to rest that day, not that I thought she would need it, but because I didn't want her to overdo it as we would have a late night and I knew Saturday was usually her shopping day so if she conserved her energy it might help her survive the night out.

We arrived at the restaurant near the theatre, where I had booked a table for dinner before the show. It was nothing too fancy, just a Italian restaurant. We decided we would just have soft drinks with our meal and ordered seven small dishes to share between us. The service was quick and the meal was delicious. I'd brought Mum there a few times, and each time it had always been the same, which was why I'd thought it would be ideal for tonight.

After dinner, we went to the theatre. I had arranged VIP tickets for her to meet the band and a special place for her to sit so that she didn't need to worry about other people getting in her way. The look on her face when I said we were going to meet the band was priceless. She just kept opening her mouth as if to speak, then closing it, then opening it again. Eventually she managed to squeak out the word 'really?' with her eyes wide open. I was glad I told her just after we finished dinner because if I'd told her before, I don't think she would have been able to eat anything.

Working our way backstage, I held our passes up to the security man that was standing by. He let us in and hollered to one of the other staff that we had guest passes. A young lad in a theatre uniform came to get us.

"Hi, my name is Tony. You must be Connor and Dawn?"

"Hi, Tony," I replied. Meanwhile, Dawn stood there looking confused.

"I am here to show you where to go and to help you with anything you might need tonight." He took us to a tired-looking room backstage with theatre posters on the wall. There were a few chairs dotted around the room, and in the corner was a tall, round old bar table on which was a tray with a large bottle of water and six glasses on it.

"Can I get you some water or anything to drink while you are waiting?" Tony asked.

"No, thank you," Dawn replied. "But is it okay if I take a seat?"

"Of course, please." Tony showed her to a seat whilst checking to make sure I didn't want a drink.

I shook my head.

"The band will be along shortly."

No sooner had he said that than the door opened and in walked the lead singer, who was also one of the best men in the entertainment industry I knew. Well, I only really knew a handful, but he was the best of them, mainly because he'd helped sort out tonight for me. As I looked over at Dawn she was sitting there stock-still staring at Aaron. She wasn't blinking or moving a muscle. If my hand hadn't been on her shoulder to feel her body moving up and down, I would have wondered whether or not she was actually breathing.

"Look who the cat dragged in. Connor! Long time no see. And who is this beautiful woman you have brought with you?" That was Aaron for you; a genuine flirt.

"Give it a rest, Aaron. This is Dawn."

"Man, it has been so long. You have been too busy keeping the criminals locked up."

"And you have been busy singing to my girlfriend every time she turns her music on."

"Well someone has to do it." Aaron walked over to Dawn, who had unfrozen herself and was now looking curiously at our exchange.

"You didn't tell me you knew each other?" she said to me.

"I thought I would surprise you," I replied.

"Well, you certainly have done that," she said, putting her hand out ready to shake Aaron's hand. Aaron moved her hand away and gave her a hug instead.

"It is lovely to meet you, Dawn. I might not have seen this reprobate for a while, but he has managed to communicate with me and tell me how lucky he is to have found you, and I want to thank you for saving all womankind by taking him off the market."

She laughed shyly. "How do you know each other?"

"I could come up with a really glamourous answer to that, but I don't think you would believe it."

"Aaron's dad was a police officer, and he served with my dad and Alan. That's how we met."

"Oh, did you live in Greengrove? I am sorry I don't remember you."

"No, I didn't live in Greengrove. I went to live with my mum in London and only saw my dad every other weekend and on holidays, but when I used to visit him, I'd also see Connor and Alan."

"Oh, so you know Alan as well?"

"Oh yes, Alan is my godfather. That's why Connor and I used to meet up. In fact, I'm hoping to pop round and see him tomorrow before we move on again to another venue."

"Where's the rest of the band?" Connor asked.

"Why, did you miss us?" a voice said as the three remaining members of the band came through the door. Aaron made the introductions.

"Dawn, may I introduce you to Chase, Declan, and Killian. Guys, this is Connor's girlfriend, Dawn."

All the band walked over and gave Dawn a hug and a kiss on the cheek, then Tony popped his head round the door and gave everyone a ten-minute warning.

"We'd better get ready, and you two better get to your seats. I think Tony is taking you to them. Afterwards, Tony will bring you back here and we can finish catching up."

Aaron and the band left the room and Dawn and I followed Tony to our seats. I had no idea where it was because Aaron had arranged it all for me. It seemed he'd placed us in our very own seating area just off the wings! It was nowhere near were people were running or where we could be in the way. We had a view of everything, and it wasn't too loud. I couldn't have managed this on my own if I had tried.

When Dawn realised where we were sitting, she was as blown over as I was. Before Tony left us, he checked to make sure we didn't need anything and promised that he would be back in the interval.

Dawn turned round to me and asked, "Did you know we were going to be sitting here?"

"I'm just as surprised as you! I phoned Aaron and he said he would arrange everything. I really wasn't expecting anything like this."

"Remind me to put you in charge of organising things every time we go out, because I really am having a wonderful time, thank you."

She leaned over and kissed me, and either the warm-up

band had started or her kiss started a drum roll going off in my head. As these weren't theatre seats—they were just normal chairs that you would find in a conference room—we could sit a lot closer to each other. I had my arm around Dawn's shoulders, and she was leaning against me, holding onto my other hand as we enjoyed watching and listening to the music of the warm-up band.

Forty-five minutes later, Tony re-appeared to see if we wanted any drinks. We both just asked for some water, which he went to get. We sat and watched everyone in the auditorium during the break go and get their drinks, most people coming back with pints and little bottles of wine to drink during the show. Soon enough, the lights flashed on and off, and in the blackness of the stage was the outline of someone getting ready to play the drums.

As the lights flashed, the drums began to beat, DU-DUM. The flashes got faster, DU-DUM, DU-DUM, and then two guitarists joined in, and the music flowed as the lights on stage lit up on everyone's faces, and the band's first song started. After they had finished the first song, Aaron welcomed everyone and introduced the other band members, who each did a little bit of a solo. The band then continued playing all their favourites until they had nearly finished their set.

All of a sudden, Aaron said, "The next song I would

like to dedicate to a wonderful woman called Dawn. She has captured the heart of my best friend, and that is not an easy thing to do. She needs all the luck in the world, and I'm hoping my friend since childhood will help me sing this song … although he might need a bit of persuasion. So while Killian goes and gets him, I want to hear everyone shout his name! Are you ready? On three. One, two, three, Connor!"

My name echoed around the room. I looked over to Dawn, who was laughing so much she had tears in her eyes.

"I'm going to kill him!" I grumbled.

She turned to me and said, "Your public awaits," by which time Killian arrived and said, "Shall we? You know resistance is futile."

"Did you know he was going to do this?"

"Of course we did!"

"You could have given me a heads up!"

"Now where would the fun be in that?"

I conceded that I was going to get up on the stage, but when Aaron and I were alone I was going to have a few words with my friend, and I swore to myself that one day I was going to get my own back. As I walked up on stage, Aaron reached his hand out to shake it as if I hadn't seen him an hour ago.

"I'm going to get my own back one day. You'll see," I muttered to him.

He just laughed. I was trying to put on a brave face, but I was mortified. My heart dropped into stomach. I hated being the centre of attention. I was trying to loosen up, because I knew that I was as stiff as anything, and that wouldn't help with singing and the audience had paid money to hear the band not to see this pitiful sight. Taking a deep breath I looked over towards Dawn and she blew me a kiss. Suddenly all my tension went away.

He introduced me to the crowd and the song we were singing, an old song we used to sing together called Dreamers Dream which was on the first record the band released. Luckily, there weren't many parts for me to remember as I just sang the chorus with the rest of the band. When the song had finished, I couldn't wait to get off the stage.

Aaron took to the microphone again. "Connor, everyone." Everyone shouted and screamed my name.

I just lifted my hand up awkwardly and waved while I left the stage, heading back to Dawn, who was standing up and clapping. When I reached her, she said, "You did brilliantly!"

"Don't you dare say any more! That was awful! I hated every minute of it."

"Well, I still think you're amazing. Now hush, it's their last song, and you need to think about your revenge."

The boys sang their last song then came back on the stage for an encore. Meanwhile, Tony came and took us back to the room to wait for the band. Twenty minutes later, they arrived. Aaron was wearing a female fancy dress mask and a pair of glasses.

Dawn asked Killian why he was wearing them, and Killian's reply said it all. "He knows that Connor wouldn't hit a woman, let alone a woman wearing glasses!"

"Except we all know Connor prefers gentle revenge, which is best served up cold," she replied.

Walking over to Aaron, I grabbed hold of the glasses and pulled the mask off his face. "Don't be so stupid. I'm not going to hit you … this time … although you pull that again and I might just think about it. You know I hate being on the stage!"

His face looked full of remorse, although his eyes were still shining bright. "It was worth it, though! I mean … I am so very sorry."

"No, you're not. You would do it again if you could."

"That's true. Am I forgiven?"

"Yes, okay, although I will get my own back on you, mark my words."

"I believe you."

We stayed chatting with the band for another half an hour before we had to get home. It has half past eleven, and it would be past midnight before we got home, and I could see the energy draining from Dawn. No sooner had we got in the car than she had fallen asleep. Hopefully the thirty minutes it would take for us to get home would replenish her energy enough to get in the house and get ready for bed. Waking her up wasn't easy as I parked in her drive. I did think about carrying her into her house asleep, but I worried about her waking up and being frightened while I carried her, so I thought it would be best if I woke her up.

Dawn was still dozy. I helped her into the house and into her room. While I went and locked everything up, she went to the bathroom and brushed her teeth and got ready for bed, so by the time I came back to the room, she was just climbing into bed.

With a sleepy voice, she said, "Thank you so much, I had a wonderful time tonight. I loved every minute of it, and I love you."

"I love you too." Leaning over, I gave her a kiss and told her to go back to sleep, which she did before I had even turned away to go towards the bathroom.

We both slept in the next morning. I woke up first. The time, according to my phone, was nine o'clock. I had no idea when I had last slept in that late. I didn't want to disturb Dawn, who was still sleeping, so I just lay in the bed, watching her sleep, but I think she was close to waking up anyway because she didn't sleep much longer.

When she opened her eyes and saw me looking at her, she smiled at me and said, "This is nice. Can we stay here all day?"

"I don't see why not."

"Oh, good."

Just as I was getting ready to scooch down next to her, I heard the front door slam and a voice. "Only me!"

Dawn and I looked at each other, groaned and said, "Debbie."

"If we hide under the covers, she won't know we're here," Dawn whispered.

"I know you're in there," she said from outside the bedroom. "Is Connor decent? Because I am coming in."

And with that, Debbie walked in through the bedroom door. "What are you two doing in bed? It's 9.30 on Sunday!"

"Yes, and we got home at midnight. Debbie, we are going to have to have a chat about boundaries."

"Oh, I might let you off then. The chat will have to wait; I am in a hurry. I came to say I am going away for a couple of days, but I wanted to check you were alright with that. That's why I came so early. I have to leave in an hour."

"Of course. Where are you going?" Dawn asked.

"London till Wednesday. One of the women I went to university with has invited me to stay with her for a few days. Is that okay?"

"You go off and enjoy yourself," Dawn replied sleepily.

"I will, thank you. See you later, bye Dawn, love you. Bye Connor," she said with a wink.

"Bye Debs, love you too!" Dawn shouted to her retreating back.

"Bye Debbie," I responded. "Now, where was I?"

Dawn and I decided to stay in bed till lunchtime, then after a very lazy lunch, we decided to have a lazy afternoon as well. She received a text from Debbie to say she had arrived in London, but otherwise it was a nice quiet day and just what we both needed after the day before. It was only later in the afternoon that I could see the toll our late night had on Dawn.

She was walking around slower, and her coordination was off, but she was trying to cover it up or she was trying not to let it bother her. While she was sitting on the sofa I got her heat pad, her favourite blanket and I lifted her legs up on my legs so that I could try and give them a little massage.

"Thank you," she muttered as I helped to untangle some of the knots in her legs and feet. I was trying to be as gentle as possible while also effective. Thankfully the massage course I had taken when I was younger to help Mum stuck with me, because it seemed to help Dawn as well.

I was worried about leaving her if she was going to have a flare-up, so I was trying to do everything I could to try and stop it from happening. I knew sometimes it worked and sometimes it didn't, but I was going to have a few busy days, as on Thursday I would have to be in court for a case left over from my previous job. I wanted to make sure she was going to be as okay as she could be.

Chapter 8

Dawn

I was walking into the kitchen, getting ready to make a sandwich and a cup of tea for my lunch. I had managed to get through this morning's tasks, so before I tackled this afternoon's job, which mainly consisted of checking team members' work on Excel, I thought I deserved a proper break. Normally, I wouldn't have bothered with a proper lunch; I'd just grab something and eat it at my desk.

I had just put the kettle on to boil and the bread out of the bread bin when, all of a sudden, my doorbell started ringing frantically. I looked through the peep hole to see Charlotte in an agitated state, unable to stand in one place and fidgeting. I opened the door to find the normally calm woman that I had come to love as my second mum push past me and grab my coat off the coat hook.

"Quick, grab your keys, we need to go. Alan is in the car waiting. Hurry!"

"Hang on, Charlotte, calm down. What is going on? Where do we need to go?"

"No time to explain. We need to go now."

"Go where, Charlotte?"

"The hospital! Come on," she said as she leapt out the door.

As soon as I heard 'hospital', I wasn't going to argue anymore and waste any more time.

By the time I had locked my front door, Charlotte was already in the car sitting next to Alan, who was trying to calm her down.

Getting into the car, Alan turned to me and said, "I take it you don't really know what is going on?"

"No, not really. I guess that Connor is in the hospital? But I'm trying not to panic."

"As you know, Connor was at court in York today, giving evidence on one of his old cases from before he moved back here. On his way back home, he was involved in a car accident. It seemed that someone tried to drive him off the road. Luckily, he managed to press his panic button, which notified the headquarters that there was an officer in trouble, so they were quite quick to attend the scene.

"From what I understand, he's not in a good way, but it could be worse. Luckily, the officers that found him know me, and they know how important Connor is to me, so they rang me straight away to let me know. So my first stop was obviously to tell Charlotte, and as soon as we could, we came to get you. The police on the scene have just let me know that the air ambulance is with him now, and as soon as they get him out of the car, they are going to take him to the trauma unit at Hull Hospital, so we will head over there now and hopefully we will get there about the same time they do. But they did say that he is talking and he said that he doesn't want anyone to worry."

"Okay, that makes sense. I just need to phone work to let them know I will be signing off for the afternoon for a family emergency." I didn't know what else to say. I think I just went into robot mode but I knew I was holding my feelings inside. I think I was in shock. Things like this shouldn't happen to Connor. I needed to see him.

It took us about half an hour to get to the hospital. During the journey, I phoned the office and texted Debbie to tell her what was happening. Luckily, she was a nurse and was working. It was her first day back after being in London, and I hadn't seen her yet, but I needed my sister, so she promised to drop in from the children's ward where she was working when she could if I texted her when we got there.

Alan got a few updates, all of which seemed to be good news, but other than that, we spent the rest of the journey in relative silence, lost in our own thoughts. Every now and then,

I noticed Alan reach over to hold Charlotte's hand and give it a reassuring squeeze to take some of the worry off her shoulders. The way the two of them looked at each other left me in no doubt that Alan and Charlotte were in love with each other.

A strange thought hit me, or rather it was a strange time to have this thought, but I wondered if Connor realised that Alan was in love with his mum and vice versa, although whether they realised it or not I was also unsure.

Just as we got to the hospital, we could hear a helicopter.

"Just in time," Alan said as he helped Charlotte get out of the car. Her adrenaline had drained as she suddenly had trouble moving. Walking over to her, I helped Alan get her out of the car.

"Come on, Charlotte, you know Connor. He will be okay, and he told us not to worry. Let's get in there and find out what's happening. Do you want to take my hand as well?"

"Oh, Dawn," she said, giving me a tight hug. I could feel the tears falling down her face as Alan rubbed her back.

Looking over her shoulder, I noticed a police officer walking towards us.

"Alan, I think someone needs to speak to you." I nodded my head towards the person approaching.

"Okay, I'll be back in a minute. Charlotte, you stay with Dawn, okay?"

"Yes."

Taking over from Alan and rubbing Charlotte's back, trying to calm her down and reassure her, I tried to catch what they were saying but couldn't hear them.

Alan brought the policewoman towards us. "Diane, I would like you to meet Charlotte, Connor's mum, and Dawn, Connor's girlfriend."

"It's very nice to meet you. I'm just so sorry it is under these circumstances."

"Diane was Connor's inspector before he came back home."

Turning around to face Diane, Charlotte pulled herself together enough to say, "Oh yes, Connor spoke about you often. Thank you so much for everything you have done for my son, it meant so much to him."

"That's no problem. He really is an amazing young man and a credit to you. I have actually met you before as I started my training the same time as Alan and your husband."

"Oh, I'm sorry, I didn't realise."

"No worries, it was a long time ago. I didn't expect you to remember. I was just updating Alan on what has been happening. As you probably heard, the air ambulance arrived the same time as you. Connor is conscious and talking. He is in a great deal of pain, and they gave him some really strong pain killers before they removed him from helicopter. They are concerned about his spine, so they have rushed him to have an MRI scan. I did manage to see Connor at the scene … he was quite bruised and bloodied … just to warn you. But if you are ready, I will show you the way."

"Thank you," Charlotte replied.

Alan held Charlotte's left hand and I took her right as we walked towards the entrance of the trauma unit. It gave the impression of being a great glass block building that would have lots of light streaming in, not as you would expect in your mind when someone mentions going to a trauma unit. I don't know what it is with hospitals, but in your mind, you don't think of light, airy places, you think of concrete buildings that are dark and gloomy and smell of bleach, the corridors all painted in magnolia with marks along the wall. Corridors in which people over the years have driven trolleys or poor unsuspecting patients in wheelchairs. But this hospital wasn't like that at all. Everything was clearly signed, but anyway, we had Diane to take us straight to the relatives' room before she went off to let the desk know that we had arrived.

We sat on the padded purple chairs. With Alan on the other side of Charlotte, we both held her hand, reassuring each other that Connor would be okay as we waited for news.

"Why would someone do this to him?" Charlotte asked. I wasn't sure she knew who she was asking, but it was something that had crossed my mind too.

"I don't know, darling, but I know that Diane and her team aren't going to let them get away with it, whoever it was. Don't you worry, just concentrate on doing what Connor says. It won't be long before we can talk to him," Alan replied to her.

"Okay, you're right," she said in a shaky voice.

Sitting back in silence, I felt Charlotte squeeze my hand. "Are you okay? I am so sorry, I have been so caught up in my own feelings I have forgotten about how you might be feeling."

"Oh no, don't be silly, I'm fine." I might have said that, but internally I felt far from it. I could feel my heart hammering against my ribcage and I was trying so hard not to have a panic attack. Although I knew that Connor wasn't in any danger, my overactive brain was still worrying about the what if, and it was that that I was trying to shield Charlotte from.

Charlotte gave me a look over her glasses as if to say, 'Don't kid a kidder', and we both laughed.

"Oh, okay, no, I'm not fine. I'm scared and worried, and like you, I just want to see him and hold him to make sure he is okay, but I also don't want to start worrying too much, because I know that if I let my brain start running away with what ifs, it might not come back, so I'm trying to think of happy things to prevent the runaway train. Does that make sense?"

"Yes, it does, and that's all we can do right now. What I will say … and this will sound crazy … but this doesn't feel like it did when I was called to the hospital when Connor's dad died, and I am using that as a positive as well."

Just as she had finished speaking, the door opened and a woman walked in wearing blue scrubs and was followed by Diane. "Dr Rhodes, I would like to introduce you to Connor's mum and dad, Alan and Charlotte, and his girlfriend, Dawn." Whilst Diane was talking, we all looked at each other, but none of us corrected her on the fact that Alan wasn't Connor's dad.

"Hello. I've just left Connor and got his permission to speak to you before you can go and see him. As you know, he has had an MRI scan. On the scene, they were worried about his spine, because initially he couldn't feel his legs, but it has shown nothing up, so we think it is probably the bruising and shock that was causing the discomfort for him and affecting the messages in his brain but that has sorted itself out now. He can now feel everything, so this has backed that up. He has no serious injuries, but we are worried about his heart rate because it is fairly erratic. Can I ask you, does your son have any history or problems with his heart?"

"No, none whatsoever. Connor has always been a fit, healthy boy throughout childhood and adulthood. In fact, as well as being a serving police officer, he runs triathlons."

"Thank you, that's what Connor said as well, but sometimes parents can point to something that happened in childhood that the patient doesn't know about or remember. What about you and your husband's family history with your hearts?"

Charlotte, who was starting to get a bit of colour back in her face, suddenly started to look as white as a sheet again.

Alan took it upon himself to explain. "Connor's dad, Charlotte's first husband, was my best friend and partner in the force. He died of a heart attack when Connor was about five. We were chasing some burglars when all of a sudden he turned ashen and clutched his chest. There was nothing anyone could do; he was pronounced dead at the scene. The post-mortem said that he'd had a heart attack."

"Okay, thank you. We want to keep an eye on his heartrate and on some of the swelling, especially around his face. The plan currently is to move him to a ward and keep him in hospital for a few days to monitor him, but from everything we have learnt from Connor and yourselves, I am confident that everything will just be for observation and that his fluctuating heart rate is due to the pain, adrenalin, and stress of the accident, as he keeps himself in great shape, he attends all his medical appointments, and all the tests I have done so far have come back clear. Do you have any questions?"

We all looked at each other before Alan answered, "No. Thank you so much for taking the time to talk to us, Doctor; we really appreciate it."

"No problem. One of the nurses will let you know when Connor has been moved to the ward and is ready to see you, but it shouldn't be too long now."

"Thank you again."

With that, she left, and Diane turned to us and said, "I hope you don't mind me introducing you as Connor's Dad; it seemed easier to explain it that way.

"Oh, of course not. Connor is my son in so many ways. Thank you so much for everything you have done for us as well. Do you, uh, have any idea who ran him off the road?"

"We have arrested someone, and now that I know what is happening with Connor here, I'm going back to the station to question them. You know I can't tell you more than that, but if

I could, I would. You have my number, Alan. Will you keep me up to date? I will pop in and see him later if I can."

"Of course. Thank you so much, Diane."

Getting up, we all gave Diane a hug before she left.

The nurse came in to tell us that we could go and see Connor. I was expecting them to just let two of us go in, but they told us that Connor had a separate room and all three of us could visit him, which in all honesty I was relieved about. I didn't want anyone to be left behind, as all three of us were equally important to Connor, and I knew he wouldn't want anyone to be missing.

We arrived at the room. Charlotte went first, with Alan holding the door for me before he went through it. Sitting up on the bed, Connor's face was swollen with what looked like scratches across his skin. He was attached to a heart monitor and was trying to smile, but I could see the pain on his face.

His heart monitor seemed to be a normal rhythm. I was no expert, but I found it reassuring. Both Charlotte and I had been to enough medical appointments to know how to read a heart rate monitor, so I imagine she was equally as reassured that his heart rate tended to stay around the eighty mark.

Taking his hand, Charlotte said to him, "Oh darling, does it hurt to talk?"

"It's not too bad. I hope you didn't panic. I did tell them to let you know not to worry."

Alan let out a little laugh, and all I could do was laugh as well, remembering the way Charlotte had turned up on my doorstep earlier.

"I take it you took no notice of what I said," Connor said.

That just made us laugh even more, mostly from relief since he was able to make jokes and be his normal self, despite being in pain.

"There's something else you need to know," Charlotte said to Connor.

"Oh God, what now? That's your something-awful-has-happened-and-I'm-not-going-to-like-it voice".

"Well the thing is, as I am the only relative that you actually have, we kind of needed to tell a little lie."

"Okay," Connor replied, still a little bit confused, as his mum was obviously worried about his reaction.

"We had to tell them that Alan is your dad."

"Mum, calm down. I'm not mad. I understand why Alan is my dad, and let's be honest, if you weren't around, he would be my next of kin anyway. Now come here, and if you are careful, I can give you a cuddle."

Very carefully, and with a bit of help from Alan, who helped move Charlotte into the right place and helped Connor sit close enough to Charlotte without hurting him, Charlotte gave Connor a cuddle and kissed him on his left cheek, which seemed to be the one that was less swollen and scratched.

"I tell you what, son, why don't me and your mum go and get a drink and something to eat from the coffee shop in the foyer to bring back here while you entertain Dawn for a little while? Is there anything you need?"

"No I'm fine, thank you."

"Dawn?"

"I would love a hot chocolate, thank you."

"No problem. Come on, Charlotte, let's give the love birds a little time alone."

As they left, I walked over to sit in the chair that Charlotte had vacated and grabbed hold of Connor's hand.

"Are you okay, darling?" Connor asked me.

"I'm pretty sure I'm supposed to ask you that. You look like you've gone ten rounds with Tyson Fury."

"You should have seen the other guy! Seriously, I'm okay,

just a little bit sore, especially when I move, but in the grand scheme of things, it could have been a lot worse. I didn't want to frighten Mum, but it was pretty close there for a minute. I'm so glad I did the advanced driving course and impact driving training when they have been on offer, because I think if I hadn't done them, it would have been worse."

"I'm glad, too, because I want you around for a long time. Who else would I share my bread and cheese with on a Thursday night?"

"Exactly! I take it mum was in a huge panic?"

"She turned up at my door, telling me to leave straight away, but I had no idea what was going on. It was only when I got into the car and Alan explained it to me that I found out you had been involved in an accident."

"I had hoped that if I sent a message telling her not to worry, and with Alan there, it might calm her down, but I guess nothing would have stopped her worrying. I hope you were okay?"

"In all honesty, I panicked a little bit, but having Alan there and all the updates he kept getting helped to reassure me what was happening, but also focusing on Charlotte and helping Alan keep her calm. Don't get me wrong, I know I will crash when the adrenaline and shock leaves me. I texted

Debbie. She is going to pop down after her shift has ended, but other than that, is there anyone you want me to fetch, or anything you want me to do?"

"You being here is enough. I don't think I'm going to be here for long. I think the doctors are just being cautious because the car rolled quite a way and my heart rate went a bit mad, but I'm willing to jump through any hoops they want to get out here as soon as possible. Although, judging from how stiff and painful my body is, I don't think I will be running after anyone for a while."

Connor and I sat together for an hour before Charlotte and Alan returned. A few times, a nurse came in and did some observations on him, checking his blood pressure and oxygen levels, but otherwise, we just sat there chatting and holding hands. If it hadn't been for the fact that we were sitting in the hospital and still getting over the shock of the events of the day, it would have felt like an ordinary day together.

Charlotte was much calmer by the time she arrived back. Seeing that Connor was all in one piece had clearly helped calm her down, although she did try mothering him, and she'd brought him his favourite chocolate brownie and decided to cut it into little pieces so that he didn't have to move his mouth too wide in case it hurt. We were all speechless when, after she cut it up, she picked the first piece up in one hand, got a napkin in the other hand, and held it under his chin then started moving the brownie towards his mouth.

"What are you doing, Mum?" he mumbled.

"Just open your mouth a little bit. I don't want you to hurt yourself eating this, so eat it slowly," and with that, she placed it into his mouth like he was a baby.

Alan and I just looked at each other, trying not to laugh as Connor tried to eat the brownie piece that had been thrust into his mouth. Charlotte then began wiping his mouth with the napkin to make sure there were no bits missed.

"Mum, what on earth are you doing? I can feed myself," Connor snapped as soon as his mouth was empty.

"I thought it would help."

"Little bits do help, Mum, but you feeding me like I'm a baby or an invalid doesn't help. I'm okay, I promise. I'm just a bit sore, and I know you know both about being sore and you wouldn't like it if I cut you your dinner into little bits and hand fed you when you were having a flare-up, would you?"

Charlotte went very red. "No, I'm sorry, I just wanted to help and do something. I feel so useless."

"I promise, if I need anything, I will ask, but I am alright, and you're not useless; you are here with me, and I couldn't ask for more than that. Everything will be okay. I'm just going to be in pain and stiff for a while, then everything will be back to normal."

Before Charlotte could answer, there was a knock on the door, and Debbie appeared.

"Hi guys, I've just finished on my shift. The ward sister said I could pop in and say hello … but I can't stay, as visiting time is over and I am not next of kin, but I wanted to check if anyone needed anything and to see how the stunt driver is?"

I was so happy to see Debbie. I had sent her a few messages just to keep her up to date with what was happening. I knew she couldn't really answer because she was at work, but it felt good knowing that she was there for me as usual.

"Hey, Debbie. I'm okay, they are just being cautious. Thanks for popping by," Connor said.

"No problem."

"I do have one favour to ask," he said.

"Of course."

"Would you mind waiting a couple of minutes to take Dawn home for me and get her some food on the way?"

I looked at Connor, confused and surprised that my

dinner, of all things, was on his mind. To be honest, I hadn't actually thought about how I was getting home, but I was surprised that he wanted me to go so soon.

"Don't look at me like that, Dawn. You have had a long and stressful day. You have work tomorrow, and I bet you have hardly eaten today."

"Well, that is true, but are you sure you want me to go now?"

"Do I want you to go? No. But I think you need to go, so that while I recover no one else is making themselves ill, and that also includes you, Mum. I need both of you to take care of yourselves and ensure that you are not overdoing it. We all know that stress can cause a flare-up, so we need to keep the stress at a low limit, so I need everyone to look after themselves. Not only that, I think I need my beauty sleep, so if Alan takes Mum home and Debbie takes you home, then I won't need to worry about anyone."

"Okay, as long as you are sure. I will phone you in the morning to see how you are," I said.

"I love you," he replied.

"Love you too." After Charlotte and I had given Connor a kiss and Alan and Debbie had given him a hug, we left his room, each with individual instructions for the next day.

On the drive home, I filled Debbie in on what had happened during the day and what Connor and I had decided we would do when he was discharged from the hospital hopefully the next day. She stopped at a drive-through and we just got a burger and chips each, which we ate when we got home before she went back to her house.

Chapter 9

Connor

I was released from the hospital two days after the accident. Mum continued to fuss, although she understood when I said that I was going to stay at Dawn's house rather than at her house. At least she didn't try and feed me again. I was over the moon that she wasn't in the room when I needed to go to the toilet, because I just knew that in the state she was in at the moment, she would insist on helping me there as well, and neither of us needed that anymore.

I had been put on sick leave for three weeks, then depending on a medical assessment, I would return to desk duties. Luckily, the tests they did for my heart found nothing, which meant I managed to walk away from the accident just with cuts and bruises. Turned out I was an excellent stunt driver—not that I wanted to go through that again.

The driver of the car that had driven me off the road had been charged with attempted murder. He was related to the person that I was giving evidence against in court that day and had decided that I needed to be punished for being good at my job. Although he had been charged, his court case was not going to take place for another nine months, as it was being heard in York Crown Court.

I tried not to be a burden for Dawn, which was one of the reasons we decided I would stay at her house, as there was no way Mum would have coped looking after me but I think we'd misjudged how much looking-after I would need. I could hardly move. I was so stiff I couldn't do anything around the house for the first week, and Dawn was having to do everything for me as well as work full time. When I realised that it was becoming too much for her and suggested I moved back home, she wouldn't have it. I now understood how she and Mum felt when they tried to explain about their bodies being stiff and it not wanting to do what you want it to do. It was a really odd experience, and to think that they had to cope with that every day, it showed that the women in my life really were amazing, although that's probably why they were both so stubborn.

Luckily, things were getting better. It had been two weeks since the accident, and Alan was picking me and Dawn up so that the four of us could go to the pub for dinner. I tried not to be a burden to Dawn, but I was still finding it difficult getting around due to being so stiff, although the bruises had more or less gone and the only ones that were left were a very pale yellow.

I was conscious of Dawn taking on too much because I didn't want to cause her to make herself ill. It was bad enough with Mum having had a flare-up the week before and there being nothing I could do to help. She hadn't even told me about it. I only knew because I could tell in her voice, as she was slower to respond to questions, but still she tried to push past her needs and concentrate on what she thought I needed. I didn't want Dawn to do the same. Over the time that I had got to know her, I knew she was just as stubborn and would do exactly that. Well, I was used to stubborn women.

It was the first time I had entered the pub since my accident, and because I hadn't been out and about since, a lot of people had come up to us to check on me.

James had clearly known we were going to be there today, because he had mocked up a book on how to drive: 'For those who want a bit of excitement in their life.'

This was what I loved about being in a village, and one of the reasons I was glad we'd never moved away. While James was talking to me, I noticed that Lacy was talking to Dawn. Theirs was a new friendship, and one I knew all the women were glad they now had.

After a short while, James and Lacy left to go home and everyone else had been by to say hello, so we were left to ourselves. As per usual, Alan and I got up to order the food and drinks while Dawn and Mum sat and had a talk.

Alan and I were at the bar when Alan took me by surprise.

"Connor, I know that this might be out of the blue, but I wanted to ask you for your mother's hand in marriage."

"I'm sorry, what?"

"I want to marry Charlotte."

"Just like that?"

"What do you mean, just like that? You must realise that your mother and I have been dating for years and that I love your Mum very much. I see you as the son I never had."

I was so angry, I didn't even know what to say. I couldn't even explain why, I just wanted to get out of there.

"I need to leave. I suddenly find myself not hungry or thirsty. Excuse me." With that, I left the pub. I couldn't see anything, just a red mist around me.

It was supposed to be really good day, but instead I felt betrayed and lied to. I was so angry, I didn't even think that I had left Dawn still in the pub, let alone where I was going to walk to. In the end, I had a walk along the river before I went back to Dawn's house. When I got back, she still wasn't home, and that made me angry all over again, because it was as if she had chosen them over me. By the time she finally arrived, it was an hour after and she could probably tell that I had steam coming out of my ears.

Dawn

A pale-looking Alan came back from the bar carrying three drinks. "I'm really sorry, Connor left … I didn't want to order any food in case either of you wanted me to take you home."

"Sit down before you fall down. You look awful. What do you mean, left?" Charlotte asked.

"I asked him for permission to ask you to marry me …" he said sheepishly. "I thought he knew that we were dating, but it seems he didn't, and he got really angry. I don't think I have ever seen him angry before … and he said he had lost his appetite and left. I am so sorry."

It was Charlotte's turn to look like a ghost.

Alan just kept saying 'I'm sorry' as he held Charlotte's now shaking hand.

"It's not your fault Alan. It will be okay," Charlotte said, although I wasn't sure she quite believed it, as her body was shaking badly. Alan had to try and calm her down and stop her shaking.

"He will come round. It was probably just a shock for him," I said. "I don't think he had any idea that either of you were more than just friends, but I think it's wonderful and you make a great couple, so I am all for staying and enjoying a nice dinner together. So let me go and order the food while you to sit and talk, okay?"

"Thank you," Charlotte replied as she took Alan's hand, and with that I got up and went to the bar to give them some privacy.

I was livid with Connor, but I was determined that he wasn't going to ruin tonight. I ordered the food and stayed chatting to some of the locals who were propping up the bar so that Alan and Charlotte could have some time together. Alan didn't need to feel bad. Connor was a grown man and his mum deserved to be happy. I knew that Alan had made his mum happy and cherished for many years.

I had just spied our food being taken to our table, so I went to join them again. I noticed that they were both looking much better.

"This looks great as always. I'm glad we're staying for dinner. Thank you again, Dawn."

"No problem. You know Connor. He's not normally like this. He will calm down."

"I know. Alan and I have talked about it, and I have accepted Alan's marriage proposal, but we are going to wait until Connor has accepted that we are in a relationship. Neither of us realised that he didn't know … but I think that is both of our faults, because we never officially came out and said anything … Alan has just always been there. I guess, in Connor's eyes, nothing ever changed, but for us it did."

"If it's not too personal, how long have you been a couple?"

"It was ten years ago today that we went on our first date. Before then, as you know, we were friends. It was a very difficult decision for both of us because we didn't want to lose all those years of friendship. We especially didn't want our relationship to affect Connor as he was growing up, because he had already lost his dad and he saw Alan as a father figure, and we didn't want to damage that."

I could see the emotion in Charlotte's face as she was speaking. It was obviously something that had worried her over the years.

"Come on, let's eat before our dinner gets cold, and let's think happy thoughts. He will come round," I said.

We changed the subject and managed to relax enough to enjoy our meal and stay for another drink before Alan dropped me off at home.

The lights were on at my house, so we knew that Connor was home. I promised that either Connor or I would contact Charlotte tomorrow. I left the car after giving both of them a kiss on the cheek before I entered my house.

I saw Connor pacing backward and forwards in front of my settee, and he turned to me. "Where have you been?" he snapped.

"Excuse me? Where do you think? I was in the pub, where you left me having a lovely dinner with your mum and Alan. And don't talk to me in that tone. You're behaving like a five-year-old."

"Do you know what he said to me?"

"He asked you if he could marry your mum. He didn't need to ask you, but he wanted to, because he loves you like a son and he wanted to have your blessing. He hadn't even spoken to your mum about it."

"Well, he shouldn't have bothered, because I am not agreeing to it. I can't believe that they have been going behind my back, having a relationship all these years! I thought they were just friends! I bet they were laughing at me all this time as they were getting one over on me."

"Don't be so ridiculous. Can you even hear yourself, Connor? Alan loves your mum and your mum loves Alan. They both love you, and neither of them have been laughing at you behind your back. They both thought you knew they were in a deeper relationship than just friends. I doubt either of them thought they would need to spell it out to you."

"It is obvious whose side you are on," he stated.

"You are being an idiot," I snapped. "There are no sides to this, and the sooner you get this through to your obviously immature brain, the better. Now, I'm going to bed. I'm tired."

"Fine, I think I will go home."

"I think that's probably best."

He let himself out my house, and I heard his car start, but in all honesty I was too wound up to go to bed. Although my body was tired, my brain was well and truly switched on. I just couldn't understand what had got into Connor. The more I thought about it, the more frustrated I felt. I got up in the end and went into the living room, pacing around. I decided I needed to call Debbie. She was, after all, my sounding board.

"Hi."

"Dawn, are you okay? You sound shattered."

"Connor and I just had an argument, and he has just left."

"I'm on my way."

The phone went dead. Five minutes later, I saw her headlights come through the curtains as she parked her car in the drive. She stormed through the front door and up the stairs and enveloped me in a big cuddle.

"I hope you don't mind, I called the girls and they are on the way with the wine and will be here in a second, so sit down while I get set up."

As promised on one of our girls' nights, the girls would always come together when our men made a mistake. Lacy, Jane, and Rebecca came through my front door not long after Debbie, but instead of wine, they each carried a bag.

"Emergency girl's night here," Jane declared. "And Rebecca has had a really good idea. Instead of wine, we are having cocktails, so in these bags are the makings of some amazing cocktails. While Lacy and Rebecca get these started, why don't you tell us what happened?"

I told them everything.

Jane looked perplexed. "How could he not know that Alan and Charlotte were in love with each other? I thought everyone knew."

"To me, it was obvious," I replied, "but because he never said anything about it, I thought maybe I was seeing something that wasn't there … but it appears it was him who didn't know."

"Well, he's an idiot for behaving like that, and probably

the only person in the village not to know about their relationship," Lacy added. "I suppose the shock made him react that way … but I thought he saw Alan as a second dad? So surely, even as an adult, he would jump at the chance to make Alan his stepfather? Especially if it makes his mum happy … and that really would make his mum happy."

"I have tried so hard to understand where it was coming from, but I really can't," I said.

Lacy and Rebecca passed out the cocktails. The tall glass was full of ice and halfway up was clear liquid and then the rest of the way it had a berry-coloured liquid.

"Dare I ask what is in this, or even what it's called?"

"We have made it up. It's called 'Men are Stupid' and it's got lots of lovely flavoured alcohol in it," replied Rebecca. Laughing, we toasted our glasses and then all took a first sip. To be honest, it was quite nice! It wasn't too strong, and it certainly hit the spot.

"Only Connor will be able to tell you what he is thinking, and hopefully he will calm down enough to explain himself. We could sit here all night trying to work out what is on his mind. I think, all you can do is wait," Lacy said.

"I do hope so, because I have no desire to speak to him until he has apologised to his mum and Alan."

The five of us drank another three glasses of the cocktail while we tried to dissect his thinking. It was nearly midnight when the door knocked, and David was there to pick the girls up. Jane, Rebecca, and Lacy all waved goodbye, then he dropped them home on his way back from work.

"Come on, I'll make you a hot chocolate," Debbie said. 'You're exhausted and need to get to bed."

"Thanks, Debbie, I love you." Debbie made the best hot chocolate.

"I know, I love you too."

She decided to sleep over because it was too late to drive home by the time we'd finished talking. I also think she was worried about me because stress always brought on a flare-up. Add that to the exhaustion that I was suffering from through looking after Connor; even I could feel the crash happening.

The next day, I received a text from Connor which simply said, "I'm sorry."

I replied, "I don't think I should be your number one priority right now."

"I know," was the response.

The flare-up that I knew was going to happen did. I needed to concentrate on myself for the time being. Even though deep down I really wanted Connor, I decided not to respond to any more texts that day. Over the next three days, I received various texts from Connor, but I told him I didn't want to see him until he had sorted out his relationship with his mum and Alan. The flare-up was one of the worst I had ever had. In the end, I had to take time off sick from work, as I couldn't even get out of bed because of the pain and the fatigue. I was having to use my walking stick to go from my bed to the toilet. When I wasn't asleep because of the amount of painkillers I was having to take, I was crying due to the pain and also because I just felt so useless. Debbie was over as often as she could but even she hadn't seen me as bad as this.

Chapter 10

Connor

Since leaving Dawn's house after our argument, I had tried to get my head around what I was feeling. It wasn't helped by a visit I received at my house from David and James the night I left Dawn's house.

"What did you do?" James asked.

"I don't know what you mean," I replied as I let them both in.

"Our wife's have responded to an SOS call to go round to Dawn's house with alcohol. So come on, be honest: what did you do?"

"I don't want to talk about it."

"Not really an option. As we speak, our wives are getting the inside story, so spill it now," David said.

Taking a deep breath, I told them all about the pub and Alan asking me to marry my mum.

"I don't understand, why are you so angry? And I know I should be on your side–all men should stick together–but to be honest, I agree with Dawn. You behaved like a little child," James said.

"I agree. Sorry, mate," David said.

"You better fix this and work out why you are so angry, because from where we are standing, you really are in the wrong."

They left after a few drinks to go and pick their women up. I was glad Dawn was not on her own but I knew they were right. I did need to work out why I was so angry.

Three days later, I was no longer angry, just confused … so I arranged to meet Alan in the pub for a drink, but before I went, I knew I needed to see my mum. It wasn't going to be easy, but I needed to eat humble pie. I eventually realised that the guys were right and I was wrong and what Dawn had said was true. I was an idiot, I had been behaving like a five year old, and even now I wasn't sure why and I had no excuse for it. I had texted Dawn a few times, but she'd made it very clear that she didn't want to hear from me until I had grown up and sorted things out between Alan and Mum.

I let myself into Mum's house as usual, although I was nervous. She knew I was coming, but I started to second-guess myself. Should I have knocked on the door rather than just letting myself in? This is silly, I told myself. Taking a deep breath, I called "Mum?" to find out which part of the house she was in.

"I'm in the kitchen," came her reply.

Walking towards the kitchen, I held before me the bunch of flowers that I had brought her.

"Hi, I bought you these." I walked over as I kissed her on the cheek. "If you sit down, I will get the vase, pop some water in, and bring you the scissors and you can arrange them while I make the tea," I continued.

I could tell Mum was still cross with me. She had the forced smile on her face that she use to wear when she was trying to pretend that she wasn't disappointed by something that I had done. As I had gotten older and I recognised that look, it used to break my heart more than if she had actually said the words 'I am disappointed in you'.

"Okay." Her curt one-worded answer showed it wasn't going to be as easy as I'd thought it would be.

We sat at the kitchen table, Mum arranging her flowers and me playing with my mug. I thought it was best if I started off by apologising.

"I am so sorry for the other day, Mum."

"So you should be. You left Dawn sitting in the pub while you took off, and you didn't think how she was feeling at all. Let alone how upset Alan was after everything he has done for you over the years, and how much he loves you. Then there's me. I didn't deserve that either." She raised her eyebrows as I sighed.

"None of us around that table the other day deserved your behaviour, and for the first time ever, I was ashamed of you. I didn't even know Alan was going to ask me to marry him now. We had talked about it many times over the years, but each time we'd discounted it because of you and the only time we don't talk about it, you ruined it because of your response. You ruined his plans to get down on one knee and do it properly. I have never seen him look so shocked."

"I'm ashamed of myself too," I said, looking at my feet. "After I calmed down and actually thought about it, I didn't even know why I was so angry. I'm so sorry. I'm going to see Alan afterwards so that I can apologise to him. Then hopefully Dawn might talk to me."

"Are you just apologising because Dawn isn't talking to you?"

"No, not at all! I really am sorry. I wish I had a reason for why I was so angry, but I don't. I want you to be happy, and I can't think of a better person for you than Alan. He really has been like a father to me. I just didn't realise that you two were more than friends … so when he asked me if he could marry you, I thought it was a joke, but then I realised he wasn't joking, and I just couldn't understand why he would want to marry you now after all these years as your friend."

"I love you because you are my son, but the other day

you acted like a spoilt child. I will forgive you, because I think you were taken by surprise and that is why you reacted the way you did, but let me tell you something. The only other man I have loved enough to marry was your father, and after he died, I didn't think I could ever love like that ever again. When Alan and I realised we loved each other more than friends, we did everything we could to try and stop it, but there was nothing we could do. We talked and talked for so long about you and how we could protect you from being affected if anything went wrong in our relationship. Every time he went out on duty, I worried that, like your dad, he wasn't going to come back. But when you decided to follow in your dad's footsteps, I could relax knowing you would keep each other safe."

"I didn't know any of that. I would have been fine if you'd just told me …"

"I guess your initial response makes sense. We should have told you and known that you could handle it. But … now that you realise he wasn't joking, how do you feel about it?"

"Well … I'm a bit confused as it's so new to me … but if he makes you happy, then I think it's wonderful … and that's what I should have said straight away. I hope you can forgive me."

She smiled, her eyes shiny with tears. "Of course, my boy, and if Alan does ask me to marry him and we do get married, I want you to give me away."

A tear fell down my cheek. "I would be honoured to, Mum. I am so sorry."

"I know, but I also know that you really upset Alan. After everything he has ever done for you and for all the times he has been there for you, I hope you can come up with a better reason than 'I was shocked' before you see him. I think he feels bereft, like you disapprove of him, and I don't think he would appreciate flowers as much as I do."

"I really didn't mean to hurt him or anyone, to be honest," I sighed. "I'd better go and face the music."

"Just remember: he loves you, and always has, like you are his own."

With my stomach still twisted up, I left Mum's house to go and do one of the hardest things I had ever done. I kept going over in my head what I needed to say, but nothing seemed good enough, and by the time I got to the pub, I still had no idea how to make this right.

Entering the pub, I saw Alan sitting at a table for two in the corner away from everyone. His shoulders where hunched over and he was staring into a glass of what looked like lemonade. It was as if the life had been zapped out of him.

I did that to him.

I was so ashamed of myself, and it was then that everything Mum and Dawn had said hit me. I knew what I had to say. Walking over to the bar, I got my drink and went to join him. Sitting down, I took a deep breath, and Alan looked up and gave me a small smile that didn't reach his eyes. I could tell it was a struggle for him, which just made me feel even worse.

"I know 'Sorry' is not going to make what I said and did go away, and it has taken me a few days to understand why I had such a bad reaction to the best man I know and the only father figure I can remember asking me something that should have made me so happy. I should have jumped at the chance of having you as my stepfather and said yes straight away instead of behaving like an idiot and walking off and upsetting everyone. I've been to see Mum and I've apologised, but up until ten minutes ago, I still couldn't understand why I was so angry about you wanting to marry Mum. But I understand it now, and I am ashamed to say it was because I was worried that our relationship would change … which is silly, because the more I think about it, the more I see that you are my dad and have always been my dad since the day my real dad died, so really, I think I was worried I was going to lose my dad again. I may not be a kid anymore, but I still need you as my dad in my life."

I took a deep breath and waited for him to reply, my heart thumping in my chest. He slowly looked up at me, tears in his eyes.

"It's the same for me. You have always been my son. I've been so frightened through the years that one day you would turn on me and shout at me, "You're not my dad.' That would have killed me. But you never did, and for that I am so grateful. Your mum and I thought you knew that we had been dating all this time, although we never flaunted it – we just didn't feel the need to, but it wasn't kept secret. All the signs were there." He looked at me with that familiar twinkle in his eye. "I thought you were a good detective! Did you ever even notice that any cards that came for us were always written to Charlotte and Alan?"

I slowly shook my head. How could I have missed that?

"I have wanted to marry your mum for so long," Alan continued, "but I wanted it to be the right time, and now that you are back in Greengrove and in love and I'm a couple of years off retiring … now is the time."

"I think I need to hand in my resignation … I more I think about it, the more clues I must have missed over the years. I guess if you're not looking for them, you won't find them."

"Connor, I forgive you for the other day, but nothing is going to change in our relationship – you and me - only that I really will be your dad. But only if you agree. Can I ask your mum to marry me?"

"Yes, of course you can, Dad."

With those five words, Alan's true smile was back on his face, his eyes shining. I knew I wasn't entirely forgiven just yet—it would take a while for him to get over the hurt caused by my actions—but hopefully this was a start, and Mum would get to marry the man who had been there for her through thick and thin, good times and bad.

We finished our drinks whilst talking about different subjects, such as work, football, my injuries, and what we were planning on doing in the afternoon. Although it was what we used to do before my temper tantrum (if we can call it that), it was a little bit awkward, but all we could do was keep trying to find a new normal. I was hoping to talk to Dawn, but I needed to ring her first, because other than a few texts, I hadn't really had much of a conversation with her. She was quite rightly cross with the way I had spoken to her.

We both left the pub, and after a quick hug and slap on the back, we went our separate ways. I sent Dawn a text to find out what she was doing in the hopes that I could pop round, but she was out with Debbie, so I asked her if I could pop round later when she was home and she said she would let me know. So in the end, I went for a walk, as running was still out of the question because of the accident.

Now that everything had been resolved with Mum and

Alan, I felt a heavy weight lift from me. I had known all along I was in the wrong, and now I knew the reason behind my reaction, which helped as well. I just needed to talk to Dawn and apologise to her.

On my walk, I saw Lily and May sitting on one of the benches along by the river. As it was a nice day, I could understand why they wanted to just sit there watching the river go by. I had a quick chat with them, discussing my injuries after the accident, when my phone beeped with a text from Dawn saying that I could pop round. After saying goodbye to Mum's friends, I walked back to Dawn's house, ready to eat yet more humble pie.

Dawn

Connor had told me he was going to see his Mum and Alan. I was still angry with him due to the way he had spoken to me. I couldn't really put into words how mad he'd made me that night. His daily texts didn't really say much about how he was feeling about his mum and Alan's relationship. It was just things like 'morning how are you?' 'I am thinking of you!' 'Hope you're not doing too much' and things like that, which helped to calm the anger I was feeling towards him, but I knew we needed to talk because he just couldn't act like that. It wasn't going to be easy – I hated confrontation – and I was going through a fibromyalgia flare-up. Debbie and I had to go round the supermarket with her pushing me in a wheelchair because there was no way I could manage walking around. I hadn't left the house since our argument, and Debbie thought it was important that I go out and get some fresh air. That's putting it mildly—she came into my room, tidied up, got me out of bed and into the bathroom, helped me have a wash and helped me get dressed before she helped me sit on the sofa.

"Right, I am out of bed and I am dressed. Are you happy now?" I said.

"Nope, not even close," came her tart reply.

"What more do you want from me?"

"We are not going back in time."

"I don't know what you mean."

"Yes, you do. You are not wallowing at home, staying in and not going out. We are going out, even if that means I have to push you in a wheelchair."

"I am not going out. I can't go out. Look at me."

"I am looking at you, and do you know what I see?"

"I know what I am."

"I doubt that," she said as she rolled her eyes. "I see my sister who I love so much, my stubborn sister who is not going to give up. Yes, she is having a flare-up, and yes her boyfriend is a typical man who has shown he is an idiot, but while he has been an idiot, he has at least been a caring idiot. Don't think I don't know about the texts he has been sending to you making sure you're okay."

"All those things are fact, but they don't change the fact that I can't go out. I am not well enough to walk round the supermarket. You had to brush my hair, for crying out loud. How do you expect me to walk around the supermarket?"

"I don't. I have a wheelchair in the car and we are going to use that. And I want no arguments, because as stubborn as you are, remember I am just as stubborn."

Connor texted to ask if he could come round, so I texted Connor on the way home, saying that he could come round. I didn't tell him I wasn't well, because I just wanted our conversation over and done with.

As soon as Debbie pulled up into my drive, I saw Connor waiting on the doorstep. Stopping the car, he approached the passenger side and opened the door.

"Have you been here long?" I asked.

"No, I just got here."

Debbie came up behind him. Tapping him on the shoulder, she said, "How about a hand with the shopping?"

"Of course," he replied and smiled at me, walking towards the boot, leaving me sitting in the passenger seat as I tried to work out how I was going to get into the house without showing that I was in the midst of a flare-up. The walk from the car to the house wasn't that far, but, along with an awful pain in my back and leg, I was tired and stiff from the trip out, and I knew the pain was etched on my face. I was just about to get out of the car when Debbie came round to help.

"Come on, let me help. He's gone inside with the last of the bags."

"Thanks, have you got my stick?"

She handed it to me and helped me out of the car.

By the time we got into the house and Debbie had sat me down on the sofa, Connor came out of the kitchen,

"I have put the shopping away, Does anyone want a hot drink?". Debbie stared at Connor as he asked the question before declining his offer, I asked for a cup of tea. He nodded his head before he went back into the kitchen to make my drink. He really was on the charm offensive. She came over to the settee and kissed my cheek, whispered in my ear to text her later, said goodbye to Connor, and left. Connor returned from the kitchen with the drinks and placed them on the coffee table and sat down on the sofa next to me. I looked at him waiting for him to speak:

"I saw Mum and Alan, and we had a long talk. But before I tell you what we discussed … I know I have apologised to you through text, but I want to do it in person. I am so sorry for everything I said and did and the way I spoke to you. I have no excuse. You were right; I was an idiot, and I was acting like a five-year-old. Please forgive me. I need you in my life. I love you."

"You were an idiot. I've never seen you behave like that before, and in all honesty, I never want to see you behave like that again." The room fell silent as he nodded. The shame on his face was tangible. "How did it go with your mum and Alan?" I asked to break the silence.

"Talking with Mum was hard. I knew it was going to be, but it was only when I got there that I actually was faced with how much I had disappointed and upset her. I also realised why my reaction was so bad. I was frightened my relationship with Alan was going to change." He sighed and looked at his feet. "Since Dad died, I have relied on Alan. I think the young boy in me was just scared of losing another father figure … and the closer he got to being a father figure, my actual stepfather, the more scared I became. I tried to explain that to Alan … I think he understood. We talked my fears through, like we use to do when I was growing up, and then he asked me again if he could marry Mum, and I gave the reply I should have said before. I could say I am going to have a new dad, but in a way, he has always been my dad. Oh, and Mum asked if I would give her away."

"Oh, Connor, I think that's wonderful."

"I hope they can both forgive me …"

"Sounds like they already have."

"And you?"

I sighed. "You can't treat me like that again."

"I won't, I swear. I'll treat you like a princess every day-"

"Please don't."

"I can't bear the thought that you're in the middle of a flare-up because of me."

"How did you know?" I thought I had covered it up, but as soon as he said that he knew I was in the middle of a flare I could feel the stress of holding a false front leave me. I didn't need to pretend; the secret was out and I was free, but along with that freedom came the pain raging around my body.

"You forget I've lived with someone with fibro most of my life. I recognise the signs. With the stress of my accident and our argument the other night … it's not much of a surprise. And both are my fault." He put his head in his hands. "Is there anything you need me to do? Anything?"

"The accident was hardly your fault."

He sighed and changed the subject. "Has Debbie been looking after you? You haven't been overdoing it, have you? Have you been eating properly?"

"How about you don't bombard me with questions? Debbie has been helping, I haven't been overdoing it, I have been listening to my body, and yes, I have been eating properly."

"Okay, I'm sorry." He looked at me helplessly.

"We went to the supermarket, but she pushed me around in a wheelchair. But I am shattered and in pain now. That was the first time I had been out since our argument."

"Why don't I get you some paracetamol and a heat pad and you can have a nap on the sofa while I make dinner?"

I gave him a sheepish smile. A small part of me had started to forgive him already. "That sounds nice. Thank you."

I was asleep for two hours with my favourite blanket laid

on top of me before I was awoken by Connor, who had made burritos for dinner.

After dinner, I asked him if he wanted to stay. It would be the first time I shared a bed while in the midst of a flare, but if I wanted him in my life, I needed to get used to it.

Connor seemed to relax a little bit more then. It was as if he had doubted that we could return to where we were before our argument.

I went to bed not long after dinner. Connor stayed up for a little while before he came to bed, but I was still awake when he got into bed.

"I don't want to hurt you, so can I just check - would it hurt you if I gave you a cuddle?"

"Honestly, I don't know, but I'm willing to try, as long as you're gentle."

We moved closer together, and he gently wrapped his arms around me and held me as I went to sleep.

That night, I had the best night's sleep since our argument. Connor still had a week before he had to return to work. When the alarm woke us up, it was for me to get ready for work. Slowly, I managed to sit up in bed. Connor rolled over to turn the alarm off.

"How are you this morning?" Connor asked.

"Unfortunately, despite the good night's sleep, I still don't feel great, but I do need to have a shower this morning."

"Why don't I go and make the breakfast and some coffee and come back and see how you are getting on?"

"That's a good idea."

With that, he went downstairs. I slowly tried to get ready to move out of the bed but I was worried because I knew the shower was going tire me out and the water falling on my body was going to hurt, like pin pricks all over my body. I had only managed to sit up in bed before he came back upstairs and offered to help me into the shower. I couldn't help but burst out crying at that offer. The mornings were always a difficult time for me, when I felt the most vulnerable and upset about how hard I found doing things, so his offer caught me off-guard. After he helped me back to the bed, we sat on the edge as he just held me while I got a hold of my emotions. Eventually, I could speak.

"I'm sorry. The mornings when I am in a flare-up are always harder …"

"No problem. You know I will do what I can to help. Obviously, I didn't help Mum with the shower, but I did help her with other things, and I will do the same with you."

"Thank you."

After I had calmed down Connor went into the bathroom and started the shower he put the water flow on medium so that it didn't pelt water at me and the temperature was just right. "Are you ready?" he asked me.

When I replied with yes, he helped me walk to the bathroom. Helping me to get my nightwear off, he took his boxers off, all while holding on to me.

"I am going to help you get washed in the shower. That way, you can just stand there if you think that's easier for you. Or do you want me to hold you while you wash yourself?"

"Would you wash me, please?"

"Of course."

That is what he did. He was very gentle and quick, even when it came to washing my hair. As soon as he had finished, he quickly turned off the shower and helped me out of the shower. He had put my towelling dressing gown and a large towel on the towel rail to warm up which he wrapped round me and helped me back to the bedroom and sat me on the bed, before he dealt with himself.

After the shower, Connor made breakfast while I got dressed. It didn't take long for us to get back into the swing of being in the same house together. Over breakfast, it was decided that while I was working, Connor would go back to his house to tidy up and get some washing done before returning in time for lunch.

I logged on for work after kissing Connor goodbye and got on with the day ahead. I had a few meetings before lunch but no sooner had the last one finished than I heard the kettle boiling, which either meant I had a very helpful burglar or Connor was back. Putting my headphones back on the desk, I got up to join him in the kitchen.

"Hi, did you get everything done?" I asked as I came up behind him and wrapped my arms around his waist.

"I did, and I also spoke to Mum. I'm going to pop round and see her this afternoon, because there are a few things she wants to ask me."

"That's good. Shall I make some sandwiches?"

"No need, I've already done that. How were your meetings?"

"They were good. I'm getting used to the new job roles I've been given."

After lunch, Connor went round to visit his mum and I went back to work. Debbie was coming round for dinner, so

Connor was going to have dinner at his Mum's and then come back. Due to Debbie starting her shift at eight o'clock in the evening, we were going to have a quick pasta dinner as soon as I finished work, which she was going to prepare at home then come round and cook while I finished off my work.

I loved nights in with my twin because, weirdly, we didn't need to say a single thing to communicate what was on our minds; it was as if we could just feel each other's thoughts.

Debbie arrived around four and made me a cup of tea before she got to work making our dinner, which we ate at five o'clock.

"So, come on, spill. How did things go with Connor?" Debbie asked while we ate dinner.

"He grovelled a lot and apologised."

"Did he say why he reacted the way he did?"

"He did, but I don't think he really understood it. I think it was all just a shock for him."

"Is he really okay with his mum's relationship with Alan?"

"I think he is now, yes."

"What about you? Do you forgive him?"

"Yes, I do."

"Does he know you are in a flare? I mean, he would have to be stupid if he didn't, but how is he taking it?"

"He's great, actually."

"What about you? How are you coping? He's your first relationship since diagnosis, and the first one you have been in when you have had a flare-up. How did you take it?"

"You don't ask the easy questions, do you?"

"Nope; what are sisters for?"

"To be honest, I was frightened to be that vulnerable, but he was amazing."

Connor had arrived back home minutes after we'd finished dinner, and all three of us sat and had a chat about what we were going to be doing for the rest of the week and her shifts at work before Debbie had to go to work. Connor cleaned up, then we watched the TV before going to bed.

The rest of the week followed into a similar pattern. I worked while Connor went out for a walk, he made lunch, then he read his book and watched the TV while I worked in the afternoon, then he cooked dinner, which we ate. In the evening, we watched films. I was starting to feel much better by the time Thursday came around, as Connor really was good at looking after me, both mentally and physically. He didn't mind when I had my teary moments, he just hugged me and let me get it all out. On Thursday, we decided that I was well enough to go to choir. "Why don't you use your stick? It will make choir so much easier.

"No."

He looked taken aback. "Oh. Why not?"

"I just … I don't like using it in public."

"Okay …" He frowned. "I'm sorry, I just don't understand. Your stick is there to make things easier …"

I took a deep breath. "People will stare it me - a young woman using a walking stick. Most of the people there don't know about my condition, and I'd like to keep it that way. All the questions I'll get if I turn up with a stick -"

"Okay, okay. I get it. I understand. You can lean on me instead."

I smiled at him gratefully. "Thank you."

We drove to choir practice. Most weeks we walked, but there was no way I was going to manage that. It was nice getting out of the house again.

I texted Jane to let her know that I was just coming through a flare-up so I probably might not be on top form. I knew that she was really relaxed as to what people did while at choir, but we had decided to enter the choir competition and I didn't want to let her down. She replied and told me not to worry and that she had a really good idea. Why did that phrase always make me worry more? When I asked Connor this, he just laughed, thought about it for a little while, and said, "Do you know, that is so true. That phrase always makes me worry, too."

When we walked into the community centre, Jane was the only one there. Walking over to us, she had some sheets of paper in her hand and a nervous smile on her face.

"Oh good, you're early. I wanted to talk to you two alone before anyone else got here. I have had an idea."

Connor and I looked at each other, trying not to laugh.

"Okay, let's hear it then," Connor replied.

"I was trying to think of a way Dawn could be involved in the choir competition, but not be tired or stressed out too much, and I think I have come up with a way. I have adapted a song, and both of you will start it off, kind of like a duet, walk off the stage, then the rest of the choir will sing the rest of it, and towards the end, the two of you will come on and sing the ending. That way during the middle bit, you, Dawn, can go off to the side and sit down, or you can just stand and join the rest of the choir if you feel up to it. The choice is yours, but you don't need to make that decision until the day, because I have spoken to the organisers and they have agreed to the adjustments. What do you think? This is the music."

She had said this so fast, we asked her to repeat it more slowly, then we looked at the music. I could feel tears falling down my cheeks. I couldn't believe Jane had gone to such lengths to help me.

Jane looked at me confused and said, "I didn't mean to upset you. If you don't like the plan and you just want to sing normally, that's fine as well."

"Oh no, I would love to do this, if Connor would. I was just taken aback that you would go to so much trouble for me."

Connor put his arm around me while I wiped my eyes before anyone else came into the room. Jane replied, "I am here any time you need, and you are no trouble at all. I think this song will be great, and I thought we could try it tonight if you are up to it?"

"That would be great," I said with a big smile.

With everyone assembled, we decided to give it ago. Jane handed out the sheets of paper with the words on from Where Is Love? and the places where they would come in. The choir was in four rows, with five people in each row. On each side of the first row Connor and I stood.

I started singing the first line: "Where is love?"

Then Connor sang the next line: "Does it fall from skies above?"

Together, walking forward from the row and looking at each other we both sang the next line: "Is it underneath the willow tree, that I've been dreaming of?"

As we smiled at each other when we got to the end of it, the rest of the choir joined in after that. We returned back to our places then sang then the last line together.

The song worked out really well, and everyone agreed that it should be our entry. We practiced the song a couple of times, then I sat out the rest of the choir practice, but despite this, by the time we got home, I was exhausted and hardly had the strength to get out of the car. Connor came round to the passenger side and helped me walk inside. Because it was quite late and I was already done in, I decided to go straight to bed, so he helped me there as well. I didn't even have strength to get into my pyjamas, so he had to help me with that, which set me off crying again because I felt so useless. What woman in her thirties wanted her boyfriend to have to get her ready for bed as if she was ninety years old? And how many men of the same age wanted to do it for their women? It wasn't exactly sexy. He said he didn't mind, but I still worried about it.

He stayed the night again and was going to stay until Sunday night, but I knew that come Monday, we were going to have to find another pattern because he was going back to work, although it was only on light duties.

I didn't sleep well that night. I just lay awake, hoping I would fall asleep. My body was asleep, but my head was wide awake. This would happen sometimes when I was having a flare-up. How was I supposed to get over being fatigued if I couldn't sleep properly? It was like being stuck on a roundabout I couldn't get off. I eventually fell asleep around two o'clock but woke up at five o'clock, and it felt as if I hadn't had any sleep at all. I didn't want to disturb Connor, so I just stayed where I was and hoped I could go back to sleep, although I knew from experience that was unlikely.

The alarm eventually went off at seven o'clock, and Connor moved to turn it off, then turned over and kissed me and asked how I was.

When I replied I was okay, he just looked at me, lifted his left eyebrow, and said, "Okay, well the bags under your eyes are telling me you didn't sleep much last night. Did you?"

"No, I didn't."

"That's what I thought. Do you have a lot of work to do today?"

"Luckily, no. I have a meeting at eleven and one at three, but that's it, and I'm not that important in either of them, so they should be quite easy."

"That's good. I'll make breakfast and you can relax. I will wait on you hand and foot all day, making you drinks as and when you need them, and I'll get lunch ready, then when you have finished work, we will have a nice relaxing night in and an early night. What do you say?"

"I think that sounds wonderful. I don't know what I would do without you."

"Anything for you. Now, before I crack on with breakfast, do you need a hand in the shower or getting dressed?"

"I think I might be okay if I take it slowly."

"Right, well you shout if you need me." And with that, he left the bedroom after giving me a kiss that promised so much.

Slowly, I got ready for the day ahead, and by the time I got to the kitchen, Connor had yet again prepared a wonderful breakfast. For the next few hours while I was working, Connor brought me drinks and made sure I didn't want anything.

At lunchtime, he escorted me from my office to the kitchen, where he had made jacket potatoes with cheese and coleslaw. He was going to visit his mum as soon as we'd finished lunch, but he said he would be back before my meeting. I did try to persuade him that he didn't have to get back so soon, but he wouldn't hear of it. So I went back to work and he went off to see Charlotte.

I was starting to flag throughout the afternoon, which I wasn't surprised about, but I kept telling myself there were only a few hours left of work. True to his word, just before my meeting, Connor appeared at my office door with a cup of coffee, and he also had a biscuit on a plate. Apparently May (James' mother) had made his mum some biscuits, so she'd sent him home with some for me. The sugar and coffee gave me just enough energy to carry on for a couple of hours. I was glad to finish work; it was days like this when I really appreciated the fact that I was allowed to work from home, because if I had to work from an office, by the time I got there, I would have been exhausted and unable to actually do any work during the day.

Connor made a stir-fry for dinner with lots of fresh vegetables and noodles, which we ate while we watching the evening news and talking about Connor's visit to his mum.

"Alan was also at Mum's. He has invited us, and Debbie if she is available, out for dinner tomorrow. As Aaron has a night off from the band, he is coming to visit, so Alan wants us all to go out to the Fish by the River. Apparently, he has booked their small private room. I did say yes for both of us—I hope that's okay—but I hoped you would text Debbie. We can pick her up if she needs a lift."

"Of course, that's fine. It will be great to see Aaron again. I'll text Debbie now, although she's working, so it might be a while before she can answer."

"That's great, but are you sure you will be able to manage it while you are having a flare? I know mum when she is in a flare doesn't want to do anything, and Alan will understand."

"Honestly, I will be good. I want to come, and I won't overdo it. As soon as it gets too much, I will tell you, but I want to try."

"Okay. It should be a great night, as long as Aaron stops flirting with you."

"Don't worry, he can flirt all he likes, but there's only one man who will have my undivided attention, and that man is you."

"Hopefully Debbie will keep him entertained. He won't know what hit him."

"That's true. Is Alan looking forward to you returning to work?"

"Oh yeah, he says he's got a lovely pile of paperwork all ready for me.".

"That's very kind of him," I replied with a laugh. "I meant to ask you—do you want me to come to the doctors with you on Monday before you go to work?"

"To be honest, I hadn't really thought about it. I think I'll just need to get my blood pressure done and a few other basic tests before being given the okay to return to work, so I think I'll be alright - unless you want to come? I was just going to go there then go straight to the police station."

"Okay, go on your own, but I want you to know, if you want me to come, I will."

"I appreciate it. Now, shall we watch a film or find something on the TV to watch?"

"If you want to choose something, that's fine by me. I don't think there is much on tonight."

"How about that detective film we wanted to watch?"

"Yeah, that's a good idea."

After tidying up and getting ourselves comfortable on the sofa, Connor put the film on, and just as it started, Debbie confirmed that she could come for dinner tomorrow. Halfway through the film, Connor started shouting at the TV about its inaccuracies to police work and how that would never happen and how if they did that they would be suspended. It was the funniest thing to witness although I was trying so hard not to laugh because he was getting so angry. I had to keep telling him it was okay, they weren't real; it was made up. Towards the end I said to him "I bet you know who killed them." It was three separate people who seemed to have no connection to each other that had all been killed in the same way and left in a specific position.

"Yes, I do. It is easy to work out."

"Tell me, then."

"It's the sister, she killed the neighbour because she felt that they were betraying her family, and she had to kill the other two because they witnessed her."

"I never even noticed any of that."

Half an hour later and the film finished and Connor was wrong. He continued shouting at the TV about how you can't suddenly introduce characters at the last minute. Watching detective films with him wasn't going to be a quiet affair, obviously.

Chapter 11

Connor

On Saturday, Debbie, Dawn, and I arrived at the Fish by the River before everyone else, so we decided to wait at the bar for the others to arrive.

Just as I had got everyone's drinks, I got a tap on a shoulder, and Aaron said, "Grab me a beer, will you?"

"Not even a hello? Surely the drive wasn't that bad!" I said with a laugh.

"I just didn't want the barman to disappear - it looks really busy in here. Anyway, how are you?"

"Good. And you?"

"Well, I wasn't driven off the road three weeks ago, so, really—how are you?"

"Really, I'm fine. I go back to work on Monday, but only light duties because I'm still a bit stiff. There are no lasting problems. I was lucky to escape with just a few scratches and bruises."

"You were lucky."

"Come on, you can help me carry the drinks to Dawn and her twin sister Debbie over there."

Walking over, I introduced Aaron to Debbie.

"Debbie, this is Aaron."

"Hello, beautiful."

"Hello, handsome."

"You're as beautiful as your sister."

"Thank you, and you are as handsome as all the other men around here." Dawn edges closer to me as we watched the volleys of Aaron and Debbie's banter.

"Hello, everyone." Alan came up to us, holding Mum's hand. "I've checked with Rebecca - our room is available so we can go upstairs when we are ready. Has everyone got a drink?"

"Yes," we all replied.

"Okay. I'll get some for me and Charlotte, if one of you could escort her upstairs."

"Come on, Charlotte. It would be my pleasure to escort a beautiful woman like you up the stairs," Aaron said.

Dawn and I looked at each other and laughed.

Whispering to me, she said, "Does he ever turn the flirting off?"

"I don't think so."

The private dining room was beautifully presented, with a large round table set up for six people, with fanned napkins all in place. The white walls were adorned with pictures of the village, but the feature of the room was a large window giving a magnificent view of the river, giving the impression that we were dining just above the water. I sat next to Connor and Alan while Charlotte sat next to Alan on one side and Aaron on the other, which left Debbie completing the circle and having the undivided attention of the flirt in the room, keeping us entertained as they bantered with each other.

Chrissy came in the room with the menus and some bread rolls. After coming back with some water, she took everyone's food orders.

Our conversations over dinner ranged from Aaron's touring to what everyone thought about the choir.

"You didn't tell me you're in a choir," Aaron said.

"Well … it's actually kind of fun …"

"I thought you hated singing in front of people?"

"When it's forced on me out of the blue!"

"Who would force you to sing?" Mum asked.

"Aaron called me up on stage when I took Dawn to see their concert."

"Oh Aaron, how could you? You know he gets stage fright."

"I thought he would have been over it by now, and I thought you wanted to impress Dawn."

"Don't worry, Mum. I will get my own back on him."

Just as the last of the dishes were cleared away, Alan cleared his throat. "I would just like to say, it is wonderful to have everyone I love around this table. However, it is not a secret to most of you that there is one person I love the most."

At that point, Aaron shouted "See, Con, I told you I was always his favourite!"

Ignoring him, Alan turned to my mum and said, "Charlotte, I have loved you for years, and we have been through many ups and downs, but our love has lasted. I know this question won't be a surprise, but - will you do the honour of marrying me?"

Tears fell down Mum's cheeks, which were burning red. "Yes, I will." She stood up to give Alan a kiss as he placed a ring on her left hand. As we all clapped, Chrissy came in the door with a bottle of champagne and some glasses.

"Congratulations. It's about time!" she said as she poured champagne into everyone's glasses.

I raised my glass and said, "To my mum and Dad, Charlotte and Alan."

"Charlotte and Alan."

Alan gave me a heart-warming smile.

"Let's see it, then!" Debbie said and reached for Charlotte's hand, and the ring was admired by all.

"Congratulations, Alan," Aaron said while the women clustered around Charlotte.

"Thank you. Connor, it meant so much to me, you calling me Dad. I know we talked about your reservations, but nothing is going to change, I promise you that."

"I know that, and I regret how I behaved before. I know I can't take back what I said, but those reservations I had were totally selfish and stupid. I should have hugged you, patted you on the back, and said 'Welcome to the family, Dad.'"

"We will say no more about it."

"Why do I feel that I have missed out on an interesting story?" Aaron asked.

"You didn't, trust me," I said.

"Damn, I always love to hear about you being an idiot."

"Dream on."

I looked over towards Dawn and saw tears falling down her face. Debbie had her arms around her shoulders and my mum was offering her comfort. I went to be with her when Alan stopped me.

"Let the women deal with her for a minute. She will let you know when she needs you, but at the moment, let your mum talk to her."

"Do you know what it's about?"

"I have an inkling, but I am not sure, but if I'm right, she will tell you later, but she is going to need a lot of reassurance."

"Okay, I'll take your word for it."

Dawn

Just after we toasted Charlotte and Alan on their engagement, the men separated and left us women to talk.

"Charlotte, do you mind if I ask you a personal question?"

"Of course not. I remember not that long ago asking you that same thing, and you answered honestly, and we have come a long way since then."

"I'm currently having a flare-up, and it's the first time I've had one since being with Connor … or even in a relationship. Since this flare started, he has had to do everything for me, from getting me dressed to helping me in the shower, and I know he doesn't mind, but what does he get from going out with me?"

I could feel the tears going down my face, but there was nothing I could do to stop them.

"Oh, darling, he gets you. I went through this with Alan more than once over the years. Even though I have had this condition for years, I still have moments where I wonder what I have to offer Alan. I am useless, especially when everything hurts and I am so tired I can't even get dressed. But Alan tells me he loves me and there will be a time when I will have to do the same for him. When Connor used to come home from school and cook dinner for us both, he used to say, "Mum, you show me how much you love me every day when you cook me dinner, so let me show you how much I love you by cooking for you." Connor loves you and you love Connor, and that's what is important. Yes, at the moment you need him to help you, but you wouldn't question it if it was Debbie who was helping you, you would just feel guilty, so don't overthink Connor helping you."

"I know, but it keeps going round in my head that he could find someone better than me … with no illnesses."

"There is no one better than you as far as Connor is concerned. You need to talk to him, but I think you will find that what I am saying is true. Connor loves you. That son of mine would do anything for you, as I know you would for him."

"I'm sorry to bring down your celebration."

"You haven't. You are like a daughter to me, and I don't want you to struggle with this condition. I promised I would be here for you whenever you need me, and you need me now. Anyway, you haven't ruined anything. We are having a lovely family meal, which is all I have always wanted. Also, you and I both know that as soon as the rest of the village finds out that this engagement, it will be celebrated in a far bigger way than any of us can imagine."

"True," I laughed. "Thank you, Charlotte."

"Nothing to thank me for; I have been through the same worries as you many times."

Debbie and I went to the ladies', where she helped me fix my makeup, although there wasn't much that could be done as I didn't tend to wear much, but my face definitely showed that I had been crying.

"Why didn't you tell me you were worried about you and Connor? I know you and I could feel that there was something bothering you—it was that odd twin spidery sense we have—but I kept putting it to the back of my mind and thinking it was because you were having a flare."

"I knew you would just say that he is lucky to have me. I needed to know that I wasn't being selfish in wanting to stay in a relationship with him. I love him so much, and it would hurt me so much to let him go, but if being with me is too much of a burden for him, then I would have to do that."

"There are times when I want to shake you, Dawn. Connor loves you so much. But I do agree with Charlotte that you need to talk to him. I may not have my love life in order yet, but I do know communication is key, and you need to share with him how you are feeling. And don't try to hide things from me again – it never works out well."

"Sorry, Debs, love you."

"Love you too. Now come on, let's get back in there. I want to torment Aaron a bit more before we have to leave."

Walking back into the room, I walked over to Connor, who put his arm around me, kissed my head, and whispered in my ear, "Are you alright?"

With a quick nod so that only he saw, I joined in on the conversation. Half an hour later, we left the restaurant. After dropping Debbie off at her house, we went straight home.

Settling in with a cup of tea before bed, I knew I needed to talk to Connor about what I was thinking, but I couldn't think how to start … so I just didn't.

"Are you happy that Alan asked your mum to marry him tonight?" I asked.

"Actually yes, I am. As he said, we are all his family, and I think it was the proposal that was best for them in front of the ones they love. Neither of them would have liked the grand gestures, and knowing those two, they probably talked about it so much that it was just a formality anyway. But I'm glad Aaron was there - it would have meant so much to Alan."

"He was funny. Debbie loved tormenting him all night, and he took it all in good faith. He really is a good man."

"He was dealt a bad deal when he was a child. When his mum and dad divorced, they used him as a weapon against each other, but really, neither of them wanted him. When he came here, he spent a lot of time with Alan, me, and my mum. In fact, the only decent thing his parents ever did was make Alan his godparent, which was something Alan took very seriously."

"It is clear your friendship has meant a lot to him over the years. You're one in a million, Connor."

"No I'm not, I'm just a decent individual who looks after those he loves." He paused and looked at me sincerely. "Can

I ask why you were crying tonight? If you don't want to tell me, that's okay, but if there's something I can do to help, then please let me know."

My heart thumped. I guess I have no choice, then. "It's stupid … it was about us." I took a deep breath. "This was the first flare-up I've ever had when in a relationship, and I keep thinking that you shouldn't have to do the things that you have been doing for me—helping me in the shower, helping me get dressed—and that got me to thinking that … I'm a drain on you, and you would be better off with someone else."

He took a moment to reply, a mixture of emotions across his face. "You're not seeing it my way. I love you, and I know you love me. It hurts me to see you in pain every day, and this flare was awful, but it isn't all bad for me. I got to help my beautiful woman undress, I got to help her have a shower, and I got to help her clean her beautiful body. That isn't a chore; that is a privilege. I also feel guilty because the reason you are having this flare is because you were doing so much for me when I was recuperating and then we had the argument so you had the stress from that. So it is my fault that you are ill."

"This flare could have happened at any time, but you are right … I didn't look at things that way. I just want you to know that, although it would hurt me so much because I love you, if you want out, I wouldn't blame you and I wouldn't let anyone else blame you, either."

"I am not going anywhere," he said stubbornly. "You are stuck with me, and I don't care how many times you think I will be better off without you—it won't ever be true. I am a better person with you, and if I'm honest, I need to stick with you for the rest of your life, because while I am quite good at getting you undressed, I think we will agree that I need a lot of practice in getting you dressed; it is just all wrong. But seriously, I need you too. There is nothing one sided in our relationship. I need you as much as you need me, but for different reasons. That's the wonderful thing about our relationship."

"I love you, Connor."

"That's good, because I love you too." Just as he said that, my phone rang. I was surprised to find it was Charlotte on the phone to tell me that, as predicted, May had decided to put on an impromptu party to celebrate their engagement next Saturday, so she wanted to make sure we all had the weekend free.

When I told Connor, he laughed and confirmed he had nothing on.

Connor stayed Saturday night, and on Sunday, we had a nice relaxing day before he returned to his flat ready to go to work the next day. I knew he was looking forward to it, even if it was just paperwork, but I think he was hoping Dr Davies would be able to tell him how long it would be before he could return to normal duties and training for triathlons. Although he had already pulled out of the one he was training for, he was reluctant to put his training on hold for too long.

Chapter 12

Connor

It was good waking up knowing that I was finally going to work. I had never had three weeks off work before. I didn't like not waking up next to Dawn though, especially as I knew she still wasn't well, but if she needed help, she knew how to reach me.

I texted Dawn as soon as I'd had my shower and while I was waiting for my coffee. She reassured me she was fine and wished me luck at the doctor's. After breakfast, I walked to the surgery for my appointment, hoping I would be given a fit note or at least a date as to when I could return to training and proper duties.

Unfortunately, my appointment with Dr Davies didn't shed any light on when I would be able to return to competing in triathlons, but at least I knew that he thought I would only have a couple of weeks of light duties before I could go to full duties at work. I knew it was so that the internal bruising that my ribs had sustained in the accident could calm down, but other than still being stiff, I felt fine. However, I was willing to do whatever they said I needed to do, so I made another appointment to see him in two weeks just so that he could check on my progress. I phoned Dawn to let her know what was going on before I went to work.

I got to work and knocked on Alan's door to let him know that I was there and what Dr Davies had said. He smiled and handed me a pile of paperwork that he had saved apparently just for me.

"Call it a welcome-back present."

"Gee, thanks, Dad."

We both laughed and I left to go to my office and get on with it, and that was where I stayed all day, except for a few interruptions from other police officers asking questions or welcoming me back. To be honest, I was glad when it was time to go home. I was going to Dawn's that night for dinner. I had promised I would stop by my house and bring a change of clothing so I could stay the night and also to get a takeaway so neither of us had to worry about cooking and we could celebrate my first day back at work.

As I let myself in with the Chinese in my hand, Dawn's house was quiet. I walked towards the kitchen and put the dinner on the bench before walking to the living room and finding Dawn fast asleep on the sofa.

I walked over to her and gave her a kiss to wake her up. It always worked in the movies - the princess would wake up and flutters her eyelids. But in real life, the princess woke up, freaked out, and nearly headbutted me. Luckily, my reactions were good, otherwise I would have been sporting a bloody nose and back in hospital.

"Oh my God, I'm sorry, Connor!"

"Waking you up with a kiss always seemed like a good idea. Remind me not to do that again," I said with a nervous laugh. "I didn't mean to frighten you."

"That's okay, it was nice. I didn't mean to fall asleep. I just need to wait for my heart rate to slow down a bit and for my body to stop shaking."

"Will it help if I give you another kiss and a cuddle?"

"I'm not sure, but it is worth a try."

After a little while, Dawn had calmed down, so we set about getting our dinner ready. Luckily, the containers had kept the dinner warm, so it didn't need reheating.

"So tell me about your first day back at work. Was it as boring as you thought it would be?"

"Other than the people popping in and out of the office, I was just pushing paperwork around like an admin assistant, but there isn't much I can do about it." I sighed. "I think Alan has saved all his paperwork from the last three weeks. Did you get any sleep last night?"

"I did a little bit, and I'm feeling a little bit better, so that is a win. According to your mum, we need to count the wins, especially when we are in a flare. That way, we focus on the positives and ignore the negatives. It's easier said than done, but I'm giving it a go."

"I know she finds it difficult at times even now, but thinking like that does help her. It felt really odd not waking up next to you after all this time, especially when I knew you were still struggling."

"There haven't been many nights when we have been separate since your accident … but we will get used to it again. And I was okay last night. I promise I would have called if I wasn't."

"I know, I was just worried. I didn't want you to struggle, trying to be brave."

"I wasn't being brave. Trust me, I was okay. I went to bed not that long after you left and just sat reading my book until I tried to fall asleep. It wasn't exactly the highlife."

"I did much the same when I got home. So, that crime drama starts tonight. Did you want to watch it?"

"As long as you promise not to solve the crime and keep shouting at the police officer on the screen to arrest the suspect when you know who has done it."

"I'll try not to, but it's really hard when it's so obvious."

"You know it's not real, and the reason it's obvious is because you are sitting at home and following the clues the writer has written for you. Anyway, last week you were wrong and I had to sit through half an hour of you shouting at the TV about how the woman was guilty and then in the end it was the brother that murdered the mother."

"I didn't know the writer was going to throw in a secret brother! I mean, who does that? It's unethical."

She threw back her head and laughed. "You sulked for ages that you hadn't got it right!"

"Hey, don't be mean. I was talking to Alan about it and he agreed with me. Bad plot."

"Maybe if your job as an actual policeman gets boring, you could become a crime writer?"

"Okay, why don't we get some paper and write down who we think the suspect is? Then at the end, we can see who is right."

"Alright, but that will only work if I stay awake long enough to suspect anyone."

"You will. I have faith."

During the first hour we had eaten our dinner and watched the programme trying to decide who we thought was guilty. After an hour had passed, both of us had written our predictions down on the piece of paper and placed them on the coffee table. During the last hour, Dawn fell asleep and only woke up in time for the murderer to be arrested. We both opened our envelopes to find out that we had both guessed correctly.

"Come on, let's go to bed, sleeping beauty."

The rest of the week at work improved as the amount of paperwork I needed to do decreased and I was beginning to do less mundane jobs. I stayed at Dawn's house on Thursday after choir and then again on Friday night.

Chapter 13

Connor

Saturday morning, Debbie, Dawn, and I went to the supermarket before heading off to Mum and Alan's engagement party at May's house. Dawn was coming through the end of her flare, although Debbie and I persuaded her to take it easy at the supermarket by giving us a list of what she needed while she sat in the café. She would only agree if she went halfway round the supermarket, then she would go and sit in the café and get us all a drink.

We got to May's later than we'd hoped, so there were already a lot of people there. Our first stop was to find Mum and Alan, but I was surprised to find that Aaron was there as well, talking to Alan.

"Hello, Alan."

"Hi, Connor."

"Aaron, I'm surprised to see you. Don't you have a gig to go to tonight?"

"We have a month off, so Alan persuaded me and the rest of the band to come tonight. Some of these people I haven't seen for years."

"I bet that was a surprise for everyone."

"I'll be lucky if I manage to escape here without Jane persuading me and the band to do a talk at her school."

"Once Jane gets an idea in her head, it's hard to resist. Look at me and the choir."

"That's very true. Now where have you hidden your beautiful woman? And has her menace of a sister come?"

"Dawn was just behind me … but I think she stopped to talk to May. And yes, we brought Debbie. I think she is off talking to Lacy and Jane. Oh, here comes Dawn now."

"Hey, Aaron. I didn't expect to see you."

"I heard you were coming and I couldn't miss out on another opportunity to see you again."

I just stood there rolling my eyes as Dawn laughed at his obvious line.

"Back in the real world, he had nothing better to do and he heard that there was free food, so he and the rest of the band have invaded," I said.

"I can't wait to see them all again! Where are they?" Dawn asked.

"Over by the food, talking to Mike."

Mum came up at that moment and leaned on Alan for support. "Hello, son, Dawn, are you both okay?"

"Hey, Mum. We're good, what about you? Are you both enjoying the fuss?"

"You know as well as I do that I hate being in the limelight. I've told May that she can mention our engagement once and that's it, because it's not as if we are love's young dream like you two."

"Oh, Mum, behave."

Dawn went to go and join Debbie, Lacy, and Jane. I took Aaron to join James and David. I knew that he knew James because we used to play in a band with him when we were younger, but I wasn't sure if anyone had introduced him to David. While I was talking to my friends, May came up to me and put her hand on my arm.

"Connor, can I have a word?"

"Oh dear, someone's in trouble."

"Oh shut up, James. Try acting your age and not your wife's shoe size," May snapped.

Everyone around us laughed as I walked away to talk to her alone.

"What's up? Is everything okay?"

"Of course, I just wanted to ask you if you would do the toast to your mum and Alan?"

"Oh, I'd love to. I'm guessing you already know what you want me to say?"

"Actually, I want you to say what is in your heart. I'll leave it with you. I thought we would do the toast in about half an hour. By then, everyone should be here and the food should be nearly ready."

With that, May went off to talk to Lily and left me to return to the others. During my absence, they had been joined by the women.

"What did Mum want?"

"James, don't be nosy. It might be personal," Lacy said as she hit him on the arm. Those of us who had known Lacy for a long time knew what a big thing it was for Lacy to feel comfortable enough to laugh and joke amongst strangers and big groups. Despite rubbing his arm where she had hit him, James had an apologetic smile on his face.

"It's alright, Lacy, it wasn't that personal. She wants me to do the toast for Alan and Mum."

"Ah, that will be lovely, and your mum will love that," Lacy said. "Did Mum tell you what you need to say?"

"Nope. Apparently, I have to talk from the heart and I have half an hour to work out what I'm going to say."

"Wow. Until Dawn came along, I didn't even know you had a heart," Aaron said. "It really is getting a workout these days, isn't it?"

"Thanks, Aaron, your help is invaluable."

Luckily, David spoke up. "I think May has a point. You just need to do a quick speech about how happy the two of them have made you and how happy they will be as man and wife. It's as simple as that."

"At least that it more helpful. Thank you, David."

Half an hour later, it was time for me to say something. Mike chimed a metal spoon on a pan to get everyone's attention. I stood there a little dumbstruck for a minute, and then I looked at Dawn, Mum, and Alan, and it was as if I suddenly knew what I needed to say.

"Hi, everyone. I have been tasked with making the toast to Mum and Alan. I am so happy I was asked. In my opinion, and I may be a bit biased, Mum and Alan make the perfect couple. In fact, they should have got married years ago, but word on the street was that there was this wonderful little boy who had lost his father at a young age that they didn't want to upset. But I want everyone to know, that little boy is honoured to have Alan as his dad. I myself know that you don't pick love, love picks you, and Mum was lucky that love picked her twice. So I would like everyone to raise their glasses to my mum and dad, Charlotte and Alan."

Everyone called out their names. Aaron and Dawn came over to me, and Dawn gave me a cuddle and held my hand while Aaron slapped my back and said, "You did it well, and I couldn't have put it better myself."

"Thank you."

"I will save you both a seat, or rather room on the blanket, while you talk to your mum and dad."

Just as he walked away, Mum and Alan walked towards us. "Thank you so much, son, those words mean so much to us."

"I meant every word of it, Mum. I love you both."

"We love you too. Both of you."

After I gave both Mum and Alan a hug, it was May's turn to come up and give me a hug.

"Connor, I knew you could do it. That speech was amazing."

"Thank you, May."

"Next time I need a speech, you are my go-to man."

"No, I don't think I am."

"Nonsense, of course you are. I sprung that speech on you; can you imagine what would happen if I gave you more time?" Meanwhile, Dawn was laughing at my attempts.

"Come on, you two; let's leave the young ones to their friends and go and join the old fogies." With that, May took Mum and Dad away.

"Will it be odd calling him 'Dad?'" Dawn asked.

"To be honest, in my head I have always called him 'Dad'. I just didn't want to say it out loud in case it upset Mum. But at least now I can say it out loud and it was my idea to do so, not his. Although at work, he will still be Sir or Alan."

She smiled at me warmly. "Shall we go and get some food?"

"Yes. How are you feeling?"

"I'm getting a bit tired so could do with a sit down, but other than that, I'm okay."

"Okay, let's grab some food and have a sit-down, then I can wait on you hand and foot. How does that sound?"

"Perfect."

As we got food and sat and chatted with what seemed to be a very big group of people on a blanket (James, David, and our significant others, Debbie, Aaron, the band and me), James and David were talking to me about my triathlon career, which, to be honest, I think I had more or less decided to give up. Now that I had Dawn in my life, the choir, and my promotion, there just didn't seem to be enough hours in the day to compete properly anymore. I would still run to keep fit, but my competition days were over. Jane was trying to persuade Aaron that he really wanted to come to the school for some extracurricular events and everyone else were just laughing at his diversion tactics that weren't working. It was great being with friends. The afternoon went quite quickly, and it was starting to get dark, so we decided to call it a day. As usual, we all helped tidy up May and Mike's house and put it all back together, and in return, May put together all the leftovers for everyone to take away with them.

Taking our leftovers with us, Dawn and I went home. She looked absolutely shattered. Her face was pale and the bags under her eyes were back with a vengeance. She'd had a long day. Even though most of the day she was sitting chatting, I knew that took a lot of energy because she'd have to concentrate on what people were saying.

"Why don't I run you a bath when we get in and you can relax in there while I finish putting the shopping and the leftovers away?"

"That sounds perfect."

When we got to hers, I went to her bathroom and started the bath. I found her some Epsom salts to put in it to help relax her muscles. When the bath was ready, I helped her get in as I knew she would have difficulty lifting her leg up over the side. I put the towel behind her head and gave her a book so that she had something to read. Before I went into the kitchen, I got her pyjamas and put them on the radiator so that they warmed up for her, ready for when she came out of the bath. I then went to the kitchen and tidied it up after our shopping trip and made us a hot drink before I went back into the bathroom to see if she was ready to come out.

I helped her out of the bath, and while she went to the bedroom and got into her warm pyjamas, I put the toiletries back on the shelf, dried the floor and cleaned out the bath so that she didn't need to worry about that.

The rest of the evening was very relaxing as we cuddled up in front of the TV before going to bed around nine o'clock, where we read our books and fell asleep. Sunday morning, we woke up after a lie-in. I went to the kitchen and cooked our breakfast. We discussed what we were going to do for the rest of the day. That night, I was going to sleep at my house, but during the day, Dawn suggested going for a little walk along the river, just to get some fresh air. I suggested we go to the pub for a late lunch, then we wouldn't need to cook dinner, but she didn't think that she would be up to that after the walk, so we settled on eating the leftovers from yesterday for dinner.

On the little walk towards the river, we saw a few of our neighbours, so it took a little bit longer to get down to the river than we'd anticipated as they stopped to congratulate me on my speech the day before. We got down to the riverbank where there was a bench so we could sit and watch the ducks and the canal boats go by. Dawn was right; it was lovely being out in the fresh air and just sitting and doing nothing but watching the river pass us by. It was starting to get a little bit cold, but neither of us really wanted to move, so I suggested that I walk to Fish by the River to get some takeaway coffees so we could sit for longer. We actually sat there for over two hours. We saw six canal boats go by, a group from the canoe club, and lots of ducks, not forgetting the countless villagers who stopped to speak to us.

When we got home, Dawn was colder than she'd realised, so I got her electric fleece and put that on her and made her a hot drink. With the radio on, both of us had an afternoon nap on the sofa, which I blamed the fresh air for. I woke up around four o'clock, trying not to move Dawn, as I was in a sitting position and Dawn was leaning on me, but unfortunately, I was unsuccessful, which was just as well as I needed to make sure there was nothing else she needed me to do before starting with dinner and before I left to go back home.

With me back at work, we settled back into a pattern. I stayed at Dawn's house on Monday nights and Thursday nights after choir, then Friday and Saturday nights. I went back to full duties two weeks after returning to work, and I had even started to gently reintroduce some of my triathlon training. Everything was getting on an even keel.

Mum and Alan announced that they didn't want to wait too long to get married and they were actually going to get married the week before Christmas in the village church, with the reception in James's pub, The Greengrove Arms. I was to give the bride away, Mum wanted Dawn to be bridesmaid, and Alan asked Aaron to be best man, which I think surprised him, but I know he was blown away by the honour of it all, and it meant I got to listen to him make a speech, after all the things he had said about me making one.

Chapter 14

Dawn

"Good news," Jane said.

I wasn't so sure, but a month after we'd submitted our entry into the choir competition, we received confirmation that we had got through to the next stage and we had to go to The Barbican in York to perform on the stage there.

We were one of six choir groups that had got through to the final stage and we had reached our last rehearsal before we went on Saturday. James had organised two coaches—one for the choir and one for supporters—but it would only take us an hour to get there.

The dress rehearsal took place at the community centre on the Thursday night before the competition and went really well. I was wearing a long black dress and Connor was wearing a black suit with a tie, as were all the other men, and the rest of the women were wearing black, whether it be a dress or trousers with a blouse or shirt. Due to getting through, we had to sing more than the song we'd recorded and sent in. We had to sing another musical song, but Jane didn't want to choose a popular song, because she thought that the other groups were going to sing something that everyone would know. The so-called popular musical songs she called them, so we decided to sing something that wasn't as popular and choose 'Somewhere' from West Side Story along with our song 'Where Is Love?' from Oliver.

I was glad Connor was staying Friday night, because come Saturday, I was a bag of nerves. I was convinced I had forgotten the words to both songs. I was also worried I was going to fall over my dress on stage. There was nothing Connor could say; every time he squashed a negative thought, another one popped up. I was beginning to get angry and snapping at him the more he kept telling me that there was nothing I could do and that everything was going to be alright. By the time we got to the coach, I went and sat with Jane and left him to sit with Alan. I just knew that if I sat with him any longer, I was likely to say something I was going to regret, so it was important to take some time away and calm down.

"Out with it. Not that I don't appreciate you sitting with me, but why are you not sitting with Connor?" Jane asked.

"I was trying to explain how nervous I am to Connor, but he said there is nothing I can do and everything will be alright. I mean, how helpful is that?"

"I grant you, it's not very helpful, but he's only trying to help, and I know deep down you know that. I think you've just got yourself into such a state that you aren't thinking clearly."

"I know, and I am regretting it already, but I'm so nervous I think it has taken away all my common sense."

"I don't want you to be nervous. This is supposed to be fun! It's not a case of life or death. Nobody cares if you make a mistake. Look around you; everyone on this bus is here to enjoy themselves, and that is what I want and why I thought we should enter the competition. Now, take some deep breaths and enjoy yourself."

"Yes, Miss. Did you know you are really bossy?"

"I have been told that a time or two before."

Connor

I didn't realise Dawn could get so nervous, so at first I thought she was joking, but when she started snapping at me, it was a bit late for me to realise that she was being serious and there was nothing I could do about it. I didn't blame her for deciding to go and sit with Jane and leave me to sit with Alan, we both needed to calm down a bit because there are too many people around and nowhere left to have a private conversation until we get to the venue. It was obvious I had said the wrong thing and I didn't want to put my foot in it again.

"Trouble?"

"You could say that. I didn't realise she was genuinely nervous. I thought she was joking until it was too late and I more or less told her to calm down and that there was nothing she could do about any of it."

"Oh, you idiot."

"I know."

Just as I was about to ask him for his advice, I received a text from her, which said, 'I'm sorry.'

I replied, 'So am I.'

"I take it that was good news?" Alan asked, noting my smile.

"Yes, we both apologised."

"Good. This choir competition is so laid-back. Jane only wants it to be fun, so I think she probably put her straight on. But you need to listen more sometimes."

"Yes, Dad."

Turning, we both smiled at each other.

We arrived at the Barbican with plenty of time, or so we thought, but everything was such a rush from the moment we stepped in the door. Due to this, Dawn and I didn't really get a chance to apologise to each other face to face. Before we knew it, we were called to the stage and it was our turn to sing our duet for 'Where is Love?' During the walk out, we kissed and made up, and I could tell she was more relaxed than when we'd left home that morning. Both songs went really well. All we had to do was wait for the results, as we were the last choir to perform, so we didn't have long.

As we were all waiting backstage there was an announcement. "Could all members of the choirs come to the stage please?" As all the choirs squeezed onto the stage, our group were the only ones that looked relaxed. The third and second places were called, and as the first place was called, we couldn't believe our ears. The winner was Greengrove Choir.

We won!

Author's Note

In this story, both Dawn and Charlotte have fibromyalgia, and throughout the story, it shows how they both handle having this condition. This story is very close to my heart as someone with a diagnosis of fibromyalgia. Writing it was particularly difficult, especially since I had an operation during that time, which had complications and resulted in a flare that seems endless.

The thing with fibromyalgia is it is not a one size fits all. It is different for everyone, and even the common themes carry over from one person to the next. So while I used my own experiences and some research for things such as diagnosis, I am aware that other people's experiences may differ. The stories of fibromyalgia in this book are not a blanket depiction. As a sufferer of fibromyalgia I know that not every day is the same and neither is every flare-up.

If your diagnosis differs from Dawn's, that's okay. If you feel differently than Dawn and Charlotte, that's okay, too. There is nothing wrong with that. Fibromyalgia is a very subjective disability and everyone's experience is different, as is their treatment. If you live in the UK, you can find good information on fibromyalgia from the Fibromyalgia Action UK charity at www.fmauk.org.

About The Author

Helen is a mother of two grown-up daughters living in North Yorkshire. History and research have always been something she has loved, and she has three master's degrees in History which she did later in life. She has always wanted to write. Due to being diagnosed as being dyslexic later in life, she always thought it was something she couldn't do, but she is proving herself wrong. Along with reading, Helen loves visiting many different places in the United Kingdom, especially if they have canals or waterfalls.

The Inspiration for Greengrove is her love of canals, as she finds them very tranquil places that have the ability to calm her, so where better to set a book?

COMING SOON

Second Chances

Greengrove Series Book 4

Debbie

I had found the love of my life when I was away at York University doing my nursing degree. Three years I spent with him. Then one day it all came tumbling down around my shoulders. It took a while to pick myself up and then when I did, I gave up on love.

Years later, away from Greengrove for a few days with some friends, I didn't expect my past to haunt me.

Toby

Me and my business partner Charles walked into the bar to celebrate closing the biggest deal of our career. Sitting at the bar, Charles looked over, checking out the talent, as he called it, when he spotted a group of women walking past. "I have found the women I am going to marry," he said. Here we go again, I thought, looking over to the group, and it was then that I couldn't believe what I was seeing. I had to close my eyes and re-open them again in the hopes I was wrong, but I wasn't. There, in the middle of the group, was the woman who broke my heart, Debbie Sims.

A Special Place

Greengrove Series Book 1

Lacy

Since the age of eight I have been told there was something wrong with me. There must be because I have no friends except James who has always looked out for me although I don't know why. There is something special about James being around him makes me feel at home if only things were different!

James

I have admired Lacy for years she has an inner strength that she doesn't realise that she has and one day I am determined to ask her out… I know that when I ask her out, she will question and second guess everything but one day we will be a couple.

New Beginnings

Greengrove Series Book 2

David

I moved to Greengrove after my divorce to open a restaurant on the river in the lovely village my friend James introduced me to. Opening a restaurant is hard work and soon I became a workaholic but a chance meeting at James and Lacy's engagement party has shown me that there is more to life than working and hopefully together we can put our pasts behind us and work on our new beginnings together.